The
Study of
Animal
Languages

The Study of Animal Languages

LINDSAY STERN

VIKING

VIKING
An imprint of Penguin Random House LLC
penguinrandomhouse.com

Library of Congress Cataloging-in-Publication Data

Names: Stern, Lindsay, author.
Title: The study of animal languages / Lindsay Stern.
Description: New York, New York : Viking, [2019] |
Identifiers: LCCN 2018029666 (print) | LCCN 2018032065 (ebook) |
ISBN 9780525557449 (ebook) | ISBN 9780525557432 (hardcover) |
ISBN 9781984877628 (international edition)
Subjects: | BISAC: FICTION / Literary. | FICTION / Family Life. |
FICTION / Humorous.
Classification: LCC PS3619.T47854 (ebook) | LCC PS3619.T47854 S78 2019
(print) | DDC 813/.6—dc23
LC record available at https://lccn.loc.gov/2018029666

Printed in the United States of America
1   3   5   7   9   10   8   6   4   2

Set in Granjon LT Std Roman

Designed by Gretchen Achilles

To my family

If a lion could speak,
we could not understand him.

—LUDWIG WITTGENSTEIN,
Philosophical Investigations

Part I

One

——

A ll my life I've been waiting," says my father-in-law, through the stall door. We have stopped at a rest area along the interstate, halfway between our homes. I would meet him back in the car, if only he would stop waxing poetic.

"Frank?" I face the mirror, smoothing the hair over my thinning spot. "I'll be—"

"First for school to end," he interrupts. "Then for my twenties, then for success. Marriage, children, et cetera. For them to leave. For their children. Then the waiting became less conspicuous. Waiting for the cry of boiled water. For the paper. For spring. It took a mighty long time to understand that what I'd been waiting for wasn't each thing, actually, but the chance to wait for whatever came next."

The toilet sounds, mercifully. It is not Frank's, however, but the door of the adjoining stall that swings open. An elderly woman advances, angles toward the sink. She has been listening. She rinses her hands.

"Sorry," I volunteer. "Men's is out of order."

Through the mirror she delivers a qualified smile, snaps her wrists over the drain, and departs. When I look up Frank is shuffling toward me, coaxing the tongue of his belt into its loop. His shirt is too broad for his shoulders, and his face appears, as it usually does, to harbor some inconvenient hope.

He follows me back into the food mart, where I pay for a lukewarm coffee and the packaged croissant he's selected. My watch reads half past five.

"Looks about time for your meds," I say.

Grimacing, he turns away, pushing open the glass door. Outside a shy rain has started, colder than it looks.

"You know what it does to me, right?" he says, as we fold ourselves into the car.

"Come on. I promised your daughter."

"Promised her what?"

"That you'd be comfortable." I stab the ignition, but the car resists. "She wants you comfortable."

Prue hadn't wanted him to come at all, in fact. *He's unstable,* she'd said again this morning, as I downloaded an audiobook—a biography of Noam Chomsky I should have read long ago—for the drive up. This was an exaggeration, though Frank has been less predictable, lately, than in the six years I have known him, phoning Prue at odd hours to kvetch about the government, or to solicit her "scientific opinion" on matters completely outside her purview. She had tried to convince him to cancel the trip, but he had insisted. She would be delivering the College's annual public lecture in the Life Sciences tomorrow, and he was determined to attend. With Prue scrambling to finish her tenure dossier, and with Frank lacking both a car and the money to rent one, the task of ferrying him from his studio in Chester, Vermont, to our home in Rhode Island had fallen to me.

The engine sputters to life. I swing an arm behind his seat, glancing back to find a Labrador between our taillights, towing a woman in heels. I slam the brakes. She flips me off and staggers after the dog, tenting a newspaper over her hair.

"It evicts me," Frank says, "from my goddamn skin. Turns me into a sleeping and eating machine, is what it does."

The Clozaril, he means. Prescribed for schizophrenia and, in rare cases—among them, Frank's—bipolar disorder.

"Like there's a twelve-foot margin between me and the world, is what it's like," he adds. "Between me and my own head."

"You seem present enough to me," I say. He has complained about the side effects of Clozaril before—the night sweats, the vertigo—but never this obliquely.

"Nothing like when I'm off them," he says. "When I'm off them, I'm myself. Only trouble is the gaps."

We coast onto the highway. To our left a Christmas tree shudders by, lashed to a van.

"Gaps in normality, and whatnot." He pins the plastic sleeve of the croissant between his knees. "In my ability . . . "

The sleeve pops open, releasing a stale, buttery odor. I breathe through my mouth, feeling the swill of irritation and fatigue he so often compels in me.

"My ability to summon the cast of mind required to shop and chat and pay bills," he concludes.

You can flush the pills, as far as I'm concerned, I do not say. While I haven't confessed as much to Prue, I have always taken Frank's diagnosis with a grain of salt. Part of my skepticism has to do with that increasing bloated leviathan, the psychiatric industry, whose ever-expanding DSM has become so lengthy that most people will qualify for one disorder or another over the course of a lifetime, making sanity itself a form of deviance. It doesn't help that Prue invokes it every time Frank strikes a nerve, as though his provocations were nothing but the illness, ventriloquized. Not since her childhood, at least as far as I know, has he suffered the pivots from elation to despair that characterize manic depression. What she calls his "mania" strikes me more as a weakness for grandstanding.

"It's not that I see things or anything, when the gaps set in," Frank continues, through a mouthful of croissant. "And it's not depression. It's that everything . . . how to put it . . . *signifies*."

Feeling his eyes on me, I say, "I'm not sure what you mean by that, Frank."

"Have you ever been to Grand Central Station?"

"Sure."

"When you walk in, what do you hear?"

I blow out my cheeks, defeated—as usual—by his passionate sincerity. "I don't know . . . footsteps?"

"*Voices*, kid." He throws up his arms, showering my lap with crumbs. "Imagine that you could comprehend—couldn't help but comprehend—every conversation taking place in that hall. That the voices untangled into words, hundreds of words, each one significant."

"Fuck," I mutter, so distracted I've missed our exit. Traffic is mounting. The detour will cost us half an hour, at least.

". . . what it felt like," Frank is saying now. "I could have been walking down any godforsaken street, sober as hell, and become suddenly aware of the wind, the vowel called 'wind,' aware of the trees and their dances, and it's not that I could have named the language they spoke, or report on it now, except to say that everything, everything, *meant*."

Through the mist a row of flashing lights comes into view, indicating the source of the gridlock: a totaled van—half-scorched, despite the drizzle. Shallow flames lap at the engine.

"You look tired," Frank erupts, clapping my shoulder so firmly that I swerve. "What's on your plate these days, kiddo?"

"I'm doing fine, Frank."

"Work? Trouble in paradise?"

"Prue's fine. We're fine."

With a spurt of dread, I wonder whether it sounds as though I am protesting too much. Things have been strained between us lately—inevitably, I suppose, given the stress of her upcoming tenure decision, though that can't be all it is. We have never been this out of sync before. Last week, if only to set myself at ease, I bought us discount tickets to the Galápagos for the winter holiday. She wrote her dissertation on the mating rituals of the albatross, and has always dreamed of seeing it in its natural habitat.

To change the subject I add, "She's very touched that you're coming."

This "touched" is an accusation, neither intended nor deserved. Frank has been present for most of Prue's triumphs and setbacks. Too present, at times.

"You'll enjoy yourself," I say gently. "There'll be a party at our place after the lecture. Did she tell you? You'll get to meet some of her colleagues, and Walt's bringing May."

Walt is Prue's younger brother, refugee of Enron's marketing team and a subsequent, financially ruinous divorce. We have seen more of him and his seven-year-old daughter than usual since their move to Central Falls. Thanks to his ex-wife's addiction to painkillers, he has full custody.

Frank offers me the final claw of bread, which I refuse. He says, "Assumed I'd have to field some eggheads."

Over time, I have learned to smile at his contempt for academia. Prue, who shares some of his scorn for the chattering class, despite being one of us herself, shrugs off most of his jabs. I read them as deflected self-reproach, the chagrin of an intellectual who never made much of his mind.

"Supper?" Frank gestures at a blue sign overhead.

"You just ate," I say, although I could use a proper coffee. We'll be home well after dinner at this rate.

"Didn't hit the spot," he says. He roots around in his pocket, producing a washcloth too late to catch his sneeze. As he mops his nose I merge into the exit lane, provoking a blast from the truck behind us.

Frank scratches his head, his white hair so thick he has to dig to reach the scalp. He says, "You've read it, yes?"

Prue's lecture, he must mean. She hasn't shared the document with me, and I hadn't considered asking her to. Public lectures are a rote affair at the College, well advertised but sparsely attended. Since my first appointment, I have delivered two for the Philosophy Department. Both attracted a modest turnout, and the second boosted my upcoming tenure case. If it goes over well, Prue's should do the same.

"Wouldn't want to ruin the surprise," I say.

The off-ramp deposits us onto a lunar stretch of banks and car dealerships. The diner, glowing on our left, looks festive by comparison. Across the road, a green air puppet throbs in time with our turn signal.

"You're in for one," Frank mutters. His voice is freighted with what he isn't saying: *I love her more.* He has probably read multiple drafts of the speech by now. Despite everything, my heart goes out to him. He has so little else to occupy his days that I can hardly reproach him for caring so fiercely.

"She mentioned she'd gloss the birdsong study," I say.

The experiment, which tested songbirds' ability to discriminate between melodies, was published over the summer in *Nature Communications*, a distinguished multidisciplinary journal. It is Prue's first contribution to the study of animal "languages," which, after languishing for thirty years, has recently resurfaced as a branch of biolinguistics. Thankfully, her approach bears no likeness to the hijinks that passed for research in the seventies—anthropomorphized chimps, sex with dolphins, and worse—but the phrase itself still doesn't strike her as the oxymoron it is. Most discouraging about the recent scholarship I have skimmed is its interchangeable use of the terms "communication" and "language," a confusion to which Prue succumbs regularly. When I press her, she usually concedes that communication—the exchange of information—is not remotely synonymous with language, that sine qua non of thought: a finite set of elements capable, like the Arabic numerals, of infinite variation.

We park before the diner—all chrome and scabbed leather. Though it is barely six, and a Thursday, the place is close to full.

"So," Frank says, after we order. "Birdsong."

He straightens his knife. The lines between his sharp gray

eyes have deepened since June, when I saw him last. His brows, set high on his forehead, give him a look of permanent surprise.

"You're the expert, I hear," I say.

According to Prue, Frank had badgered his local library into subscribing to *Nature Communications*, and would have invited half the town of Chester to her speech, had she not talked him down.

"What do you know?" he says, tucking his napkin into his collar.

His belligerence usually amuses me, but now I feel a stab of indignation, blunted by weariness. Before meeting Frank, I had allowed myself to imagine him as a surrogate parent, cosmic recompense for losing my own. No such luck. Though we have made our peace with one another over the years, each reunion reaffirms that Prue is all we share.

"Well," I concede, "Prue's team began by recording a phrase of birdsong, and then . . ."

The waitress descends with my coffee and turkey salad. Frank, a longtime vegetarian, has ordered lentil soup. As she sets his bowl before him he catches her lightly on the wrist, pushing her bracelet aside to reveal a tattooed Arabic phrase.

"Um . . ." She retracts her arm, glancing at me.

"Sorry," Frank says. "Couldn't see it."

"Please excuse him," I offer, mortified, but she is already hurrying off.

"*Frank.*" I lean forward. "That was—"

"The body as a page . . ." He rolls his fist over one of his packaged saltines. "Never got one myself. Never saw the appeal."

Laughter flares from the booth behind me, followed by infant babble.

"I interrupted you," Frank says.

Though he is thin, there is a softness about his jaw. His forehead glints. Sweating and weight gain are side effects of Clozaril. As he tears open the cellophane, crumbling his crackers into his soup, I can't help but marvel at the fact that not even an antipsychotic can neutralize him.

"About the experiment." He glances up at me. "You were saying?"

"Right." It all seems so ludicrous, suddenly—the exchange with the waitress, his soliloquy in the women's restroom, Prue's birds and his obsession with them—that I laugh.

"What?" he says.

"Sorry." I recover. "Exhaustion."

"You're very kind to drive me all this way."

It's nothing, I almost say. Instead I take a bite of turkey.

"You haven't read the study," Frank says, addressing his soup.

"Of course I have," I lie. Prue had summarized it for me. No point in wading through the jargon myself.

"So what did she prove?"

His spoon quavers as he lifts it to his mouth, emptying back into the bowl. He tries again. Essential tremor. According to Prue, the fluttering in his hands will only worsen with time.

"Nothing monumental," I oblige. "The birds responded differently to different configurations of the same sounds."

Frank sucks his teeth. To defuse his glare I add, "Which indicates that there may be a grammar to their songs, but the study is hardly conclu—"

"*Speech.*" Frank stabs the air with his spoon. "Their songs are speech."

There is a note in his voice—somewhere between wonder and rage—I have not heard before. His eyes glitter.

"Did Prue say that?" I ask, carefully. "Or is that your—"

"Tell me," he says abruptly, leaning back. "Do you give a single crap about your wife's work?"

I set down my fork, embarrassed to feel my cheeks go hot. "That's a ridiculous question, Frank."

Feigning innocence now, he shrugs.

"Listen." I lock eyes with a patron to our left. "I don't know what game you're trying to play here. Prue added a feather to her cap. I'm very proud of her. What more do you want me to say?"

Frank sniffs. To my disgust, he raises his bowl to his mouth, downing the sludgy remains of his soup. When he has finished it off he says, "You don't get it, do you?"

I gird myself. Behind me, the baby shrieks.

Before he can speak again our waitress reappears, smiling nervously. As she leans down to clear Frank's bowl her scent— floral, with an undertow of musk—wafts toward me.

"We'll take the check, thanks," I say, feeling, in spite of everything, a pang of desire.

"No, Prue didn't say that," Frank says, too loudly. "I read it in the goddamn *New York Times*."

One pill by dinnertime, Prue had said. *Promise me you'll watch him take it.*

"*That* guy"—he points at a heavy man in the corner, sitting alone—"and those guys"—a couple—"and them"—a family— "they've all heard the news, probably. So have laypeople all over the States." Suddenly plaintive, he adds: "It's a breakthrough, and nobody—"

"Are your meds on you?" I interrupt.

"Nobody saw it coming."

"Are they in the car?"

"The implications . . . "

"Go get them." I toss the keys across the table, desperate for solitude.

He stares at me. Only when I pull out my phone does he obey, trudging down the aisle of booths and through the door.

The Times? He must have been hallucinating. I wake the phone, Googling Prue's name and a few relevant keywords. But there it is, seven entries down: an article titled "Mind or Bird-brain?" published last month. Numbly, I click the link, only to find Prue's study buried in a middle paragraph. The citation is respectful, but decidedly tangential, and the article is online only.

I face the window, my reflection yielding to a view of the parking lot and the streaking lights beyond. It has gotten darker. By the diner's neon glare the strip mall looks even more desolate than it did when we arrived. No sign of Frank, from here, nor of our Subaru. As a hatchback reverses out of its spot, one taillight blown, I feel my stomach plunge. Lunacy, to trust him with the keys. Snatching my phone, I bolt for the door, nearly colliding with our waitress, who is shouldering a tray of ice cream sundaes. She gasps, catching one of the teetering glasses, but another tips forward, sloughing off its whipped cream and pitching its cherry onto a nearby table.

"Sorry," I call out, registering the sudden hush. When I turn back Frank is standing in the threshold.

"Where's the fire?" he says. As the door eases closed behind him, his bib flutters.

"Christ." I stumble over myself. "I thought you'd taken . . . "

"It's a nice car, but not that nice."

He pats my shoulder and then bends—wincing—to help the waitress clean the mess. By the time I fetch some extra napkins from the bar they are finished, and the voices around us have risen again.

"Your pill?" I venture, when we sit back down.

"*Finis.*" He slides the keys across the table.

The tightness in his voice suggests otherwise. Bunching up his napkin he adds, as though sensing my misgivings, "Entitled to some privacy, aren't I?"

Our waitress returns with the check. As I fumble for my card, Frank hands her a twenty-dollar bill.

We are quiet for most of the next hour. Frank leans his head against the window, his breath smoking up the glass. When he starts to snore, I turn the audiobook on low, relaxing into the author's account of Chomsky's teenage years.

"God's dead," Frank mumbles.

My phone trills. I pull it out to find an unfamiliar number—a telemarketer, probably—and switch it on silent.

"Cognitive science is way beyond universal grammar," he adds, over the narrator.

He casts me the steely look that still has the power to unnerve me, to remind me of what he does all day in his attic apartment, crowded with secondhand books. For all his dogmatizing, the man is formidably well read.

"I thought you were sleeping," I say.

We have reached South Kingston, and are weaving now

through the warren of roads flanking the campus. Music thuds from a ramshackle house, and then recedes. In a moment there is only fog again, everything black but the shining road and the tall silence of the pines.

"You're pissed," Frank says.

"I'm just tired."

"If it's about before, don't bother." He claps me on the knee. "It is what it is. You are who you are. I'm her dad. I'll always think she could have done better."

"Jesus, Frank," I say, mortified to feel myself blushing again.

He laughs. "I'm just playing with you, kid."

Instead of replying I jab the volume button, and the car goes mute.

He glances at me, then says gruffly: "You know I'm here for you, if you ever need me."

We pull into our driveway, pebbles crunching under the wheels. The living room light is on, and I wonder as I turn off the gas whether I have imagined the dash of motion by the outdoor stairs, receding now behind the elm. Our upstairs neighbor, the pianist, it must be. Out for a smoke.

Frank squeezes my wrist. "I'm serious."

"You're the one I'll turn to," I say with irony, though it comes out as fatigue.

The back door opens and Prue steps out, her face awash in the headlights. Her eyes are smiling, but her breath is clouding my view of the rest of her face.

"I've been calling," she says, coming around to my side of the car. "What happened to you guys?"

"Sorry." I check my phone to find I've missed her twice. "It was getting late, so we stopped for a bite."

She folds her arms, shivering. Her hair is wet, her cheeks raw from the shower. Ducking her head, she waves at Frank, but he is clambering out of his seat.

To me she murmurs, "He took it?"

"Of course." I kiss her forehead. "Now get inside before you freeze."

"Pumpkin!" Frank crows, approaching us.

Prue steps away from me, organizing her face into the look of bright repose she wears for her immediate family. Frank reaches for her, dropping his duffel bag on the gravel.

"Hey, Dad," she says.

He traps her in a hug so tight she rolls her eyes.

"Calm down, Frank." I hoist his bag onto my shoulder, squinting against the cold. "She's not going anywhere."

Two

I should begin at the beginning. Who I am, and so forth. How I met Prue. What I've published, and where. How I landed in philosophy. Facts, in short, that moor the present to the past. Together, they counteract the sense—more noxious by the year—that my progress since my college days has been a long digression. *You found a vocation; you found love,* they remind me. *Your best work is still ahead of you.*

My name is Ivan Link. I was born in 1964 on the outskirts of Harrisburg, Pennsylvania, which makes me forty-seven years old, come January. My mother, an army nurse and bibliophile of Latvian descent, married my father shortly after the Korean War. They had me late, and cared for me in a remote, deliberate way, admitting into our home none of the emotional bombast—the tantrums, the tides of indignation and remorse—that seemed to govern the households of my schoolmates. Until she died eleven years ago, of complications following a stroke, my mother and I were kind to each other. Had we met as adults, I think we would have gotten on fairly well, which is more than can be said of most mothers and sons. The same, I suspect, would have been true with my father. He was a decorated corporal, and my hero, though I inherited none of his savoir faire. A wire blown loose in an electrical storm killed him in 1976, three days after I turned twelve. What I remember most, besides the emptiness, is the slurred ink on the memorial posters tacked to the telephone pole where he died. No one removed the posters, even after heavy rains, so eventually I took them down myself. I learned later that my mother had been five weeks pregnant at the time of his death. She miscarried, and I remained an only child.

Mathematics came easily to me, and by the end of my senior year, my success in the quantitative subjects had earned me a partial scholarship to Boston University. I lived in a stuffy rented room off campus, and paid the rest of my way cleaning beakers in a lab at MIT. I read Carl Sagan. I took up chess. I was lonely, and told myself that I was free. The pleasures of collegiate life—sloth, sex, debauchery—held little purchase on me, but my indifference to them, coupled with my apparent looks, seemed to intrigue rather than annoy my peers. I even attracted a few women.

One of them, an ambidextrous Swede named Madeleine, inadvertently handed me my occupation. It was October of 1984. We were juniors, but she was older, having taken time off to build houses in Guam. I was still majoring in math, and had a vague idea of a future in some area of finance, even as a part of me recoiled at the thought. I would have made a tepid analyst. It was the theoretical dimension of math, rather than its applications, that galvanized me. Partly out of genuine interest, and partly to impress Madeleine, I had applied to study combinatorics the following year at the inaugural Budapest Semesters in Mathematics, a competitive program whose leaflet, which I had encountered in the Math Department's lounge, promised glamour and subsidized rent.

The Friday after I applied, I noticed Madeleine's day planner on my couch. She had left for class only moments before, so I heaved up the window to call after her. The wind was blowing east, raveling her thin blond hair and pitching her name back into my mouth. Rather than call out to her again I set my elbows on the sill, watching her retreating shoulders melt into the throng of scarves and coats approaching Knyvet Square. She had an appointment later that afternoon, she had said, that would preclude our habitual Friday evening date, though I had forgotten what it was. Planner in my possession, I decided to check.

Whatever I found was so innocuous it left me embarrassed. I tossed the planner back onto the sofa, inadvertently freeing a document wedged inside the cover flap. Like most of Madeleine's papers, this one was minted with coffee rings. "Two Models of Scientific Explanation," read the title, followed by a name I recognized: Carl Hempel. In the upper left corner was a handwritten note about a midterm essay, due the day before to her philosophy professor. I had offered to proofread it, I remembered suddenly, but in the end I hadn't found the time. "It had to do with this Hempel character, she'd said." Out of sheepishness, coupled with the faintly erotic wish to take into my mind what had passed through hers, I began to read his paper.

I had always considered philosophy a romantic discipline. To my mind, it stood for everything wrong with the humanities: imprecision, grandiloquence, large nouns, and contempt for the verifiable. A sampling of Nietzsche in a freshman seminar, coupled with Kierkegaard's frightful *Either/Or,* had only confirmed that impression. Thanks to souring conditions in Eastern Europe, the liberal flirtation with communism had begun to fade by the time

I entered college, and with the exception of an antiapartheid rally I attended in May I had managed to resist the quixotic spirit that newfound freedom—stoked by LSD—seemed to elicit in many of my classmates. I had satisfied my humanities requirement the previous spring with a course on Shakespeare. The professor, a respected formalist, indulged none of the postmodernist fervor—intellectual pornography, in her eyes—that was sweeping English departments at the time. I enjoyed the course. In the plays themselves I found no casuistry, no cant; only eloquent, imperfect human beings.

Hempel's paper therefore took me by surprise. To begin with, it contained no jargon. It was written in clear, vernacular English, in prose as elegant as a geometric proof.

It argued that scientific explanations are deductive in character. They conform, Hempel showed, to the cardinal rule of logic known as *modus ponens*: If A, then B; A; therefore, B. Suppose, for example, you set out to explain why it happens to be snowing. You would begin by citing a law of nature—all water freezes below 0° C—and go on to note that the air temperature has dropped below that—to –2°, say. Given those conditions, the rain must have frozen. Therefore, by *modus ponens*, snow.

The paper was outmoded by then, though I could not have known it. If I had, it wouldn't have mattered. I was transfixed by its suggestion that the laws that govern thinking also govern the material world—from the shadow on the moon to the shifting tides to the neuron that orchestrates a thought. Even miracles, in light of Hempel's argument, were not impossible. They were simply counterexamples, exceptions to natural law. After the law had been revised, the circumstance—once anomalous—would seem predictable. Nothing confounds, in retrospect.

I had located a pen and was jotting down some less intelligible, more adolescent version of this riff on the back of the essay. Madeleine would discover it later, I knew and didn't care. Here was a style of thought that promised to hold chaos at bay—that exposed, in the lunacy and violence of the natural world, the grace of a syllogism.

I stood up. Across the road a sparrow lifted off a tree—a maple, I guessed, its leaves flaring crimson and gold against the blue. Even the thrum of traffic seemed clarified, renewed. I reread my notes, feeling exalted. They were muddled, to put it lightly, and lacking in the cool decisiveness that Hempel had achieved. Nonetheless, I can't help but think of them with some nostalgia. They represented my first groping efforts as an analytic philosopher.

My rejection letter from the Budapest program arrived six weeks later. By then I had coasted through most of the books on Madeleine's course syllabus. She was intrigued, if somewhat unsettled, by my newfound enthusiasm. My former ennui had bothered her, I sensed, yet it had also given her cause to counteract it. She had played the vital one—the raconteur, the fox—a role in our dynamic she was not eager to give up. She turned quizzical around me, and then withdrawn. The rejection letter, which should have come as a relief, as it meant we wouldn't be spending the following fall semester apart, only made things worse. In the days after it arrived we were awkward with one another, like friends reunited too soon after a theatrical goodbye. So elaborate were our plans to keep our relationship afloat between continents—transatlantic letters, New Year's Eve in Rome—that their collapse unmoored us. By January, we were finished.

The *Challenger* exploded. Reagan bartered with Iran. I took whatever jobs I could, drafting my graduate applications at night, and—on my third attempt—landed a spot in a philosophy PhD program in Albuquerque. My dissertation, on the origins of the correspondence theory of truth, was so haughty and derivative I can hardly bear to think about it, though it capped my pedigree in epistemology, the study of knowledge. When it was finished, I moved back east to accept a string of lectureships—one in the Ivy League—none of which morphed into a bona fide position. It wasn't until my midthirties, when I was proofreading for extra cash, that I revisited Hempel. In one single, caffeinated evening, I wrote a paper that analogized a weakness in his model of scientific explanation to the "Gettier problem," a paradox that illuminates the role of luck in forming justified, true beliefs.

I'm gobsmacked, wrote my doctoral advisor, when I emailed her the draft. She forwarded it to the editor of *Sum*, an important journal, where it was published the following year. I was elated, but wary. I had long burned off the hubris of my graduate years, and my piddling adjunct salary had laid waste to my ego. Nonetheless, on the strength of that publication I heaved myself back into the job market and was rewarded with a handful of interviews for assistant professorships in the Midwest and Northeast corridor. At a faculty reception following one such interview—for a position in Chicago that, incidentally, I did not receive—I met Prue.

WE WOULD STILL be strangers, had I not mistaken her for someone else. She relishes that detail. I would just as soon forget it; that we owe our marriage to my error does not strike me as

THE STUDY OF ANIMAL LANGUAGES

especially funny. If anything, it unnerves me in its tacit reminder of how easily we might have ended up without each other.

"Wouldn't touch that, if I were you," I began.

She was leaning over a tray of smoked salmon, her figure drowned in a purple anorak. I was feeling brittle, after my interview, but had finally worked up the courage to approach her. An administrator had pointed her out as visiting lecturer Nicola Dunn, a philosopher of music known for her arid sense of humor. We had corresponded years ago about a paper of hers, though I doubted she remembered me.

As she turned, however, I saw that the administrator had been wrong. The woman before me was too young to be Nicola—late twenties, I guessed (she was thirty-one, in fact)—with eyes that lit up her face.

"Sorry?" she said. She was gripping the tongs. In her other—left, ringless—hand, she held an empty plate.

"It's fake." I felt myself redden. "Usually is. You can tell by the color."

She followed my gaze to the salmon, shadowed by its flounce of lettuce. The food was a favorite of mine, but a *60 Minutes* segment on its production had put me off the affordable brands.

"See how pale it is?" I sipped my vodka tonic. "They inject it with brine to keep it heavy, then spray it with liquid smoke."

She frowned. I blushed harder, suddenly aware of how preposterous I must seem, besieging her with trivia.

"Not that you wanted to know that." I stepped back. "Just forget I said anything."

But her face relaxed. She said, "I've been living a lie."

Her voice was cool, contralto. Freckles dusted her nose.

To my confusion, she peeled back a sleeve of salmon and draped it across her plate. Then, still smiling, she helped herself to three sodden capers.

"Liquid smoke," she added, turning back to me. "Now that's technology."

She took a bite. I said, to say something, "What brings you here?"—*horrible*—"Are you an applicant?"

"I'm on the faculty." She shielded her mouth, still chewing. "But I think I may jump ship."

"Why's that?"

She shrugged. "I'd like to do more fieldwork. There's only so much you can learn in a lab."

Her eyes wandered across the thinning crowd. We were in an auditorium overlooking Lake Michigan, converted by the failing light into a giant void. A single boat, or buoy, shone in the distance.

"You're a scientist," I said.

"I study birds."

"An ornithologist?"

"Yeah." She sounded almost resigned. "Lately I've been working on spatial memory in crows. Puzzle solving, that sort of thing. I'm doing a postdoc. They promised me another year, but like I said . . ."

As she spoke I nodded, grateful for the excuse to look at her. She wore no makeup. Yet there was something elusive about her face, with its long, narrow bones. Like the lines of an acrostic, each angle seemed to offer up a new meaning. I felt I could study it always, this face, and never exhaust it.

"What's your excuse?" she said, setting down her plate. Her eyes danced between mine.

"I'm just a candidate." I drained my glass. "Philosophy. Probably should have waited another year before applying, but I thought—"

"What do you work on, I mean?"

I almost rattled off the same gloss of my dissertation that had bored my interviewers half an hour earlier. But the thought of her bright eyes glazing over gave me pause. I blurted out: "Truth. How to know it."

"Pray tell." Her smile was either coy or mocking—the former, I decided.

"Your crows and I have something in common," I said, finally feeling the vodka. "There's a puzzle in epistemology—the Gettier problem, it's called. I'm trying to solve it."

This was half true. On the plane to Chicago, I had begun developing my recent article into a monograph that—while I couldn't have guessed it then—would take me over a decade to complete. In it, I planned to expose the limitations of three responses to the problem, concluding with a tentative solution of my own.

"Let's hear it," she said.

As I opened my mouth a man with dreadlocks touched her shoulder. I thought he might be her boyfriend, but then a woman sauntered up to him, her hand on his back. They were meeting some colleagues at a bar around the corner, the man said. Prue should join them, if she could. So should I, the woman told me, pro forma.

The next thing I knew we were side by side in a dimly lit brewery, shouting over the music to make ourselves heard. She, too, had a weakness for philosophy, she confessed. Before earning her PhD in biology, she had completed a master's program in critical theory (my bête noire), but she considered herself a dilettante.

Of the two of us, she was by far the more accomplished, despite the fact that I was seven years her senior. From the way she refused to break eye contact as she answered my questions about her fellowships and publications, I could see that she recognized this too, knew that I knew it, and couldn't be bothered to spare me the embarrassment. This thrilled me.

"You were telling me something back there," she yelled. "About truth."

"I was lying," I joked. She smelled wonderful—not overly perfumed, like the attorney I had been seeing occasionally back home, but fresh. It was all I could do not to kiss her.

"A puzzle you're solving?" She sipped her lager, leaving a crescent of foam on her upper lip. It looked so adorable, against her sudden seriousness, that I decided not to say anything.

"It's called the Gettier problem," I said, and paraphrased a classic example, formulated by the philosopher Dharmottara: A traveler, searching the desert for water, sees a shimmering blue expanse near a ravine. It's a mirage, but when he reaches the spot, he finds water there after all, under a rock.

"The point is that a belief can be true and justified," I concluded, hoarse from shouting, "but still fall short of knowledge."

Prue's eyes sparkled. "Oh, he knew."

She was fucking with me, I sensed, but I pressed on anyhow.

"Take this." I waggled the fingers of my left hand. "No wedding ring. Ergo, I—"

"You have a girlfriend," she interrupted, with such chagrin that my heart soared.

"False." I traced the lip of my glass. "I'm allergic to most metals."

She stared at me for a moment, and then burst out laughing.

"I'm serious," I said. The song changed. When she did not recover, I tapped my upper lip. "By the way, you have—"

"You're strange." She wiped her eyes. "I like you."

In my hotel she undressed casually and lay down on the bed. I switched off the lamp, and was drawing the blinds when she stopped me, her legs parted just enough to reveal a gleam where the moonlight touched her.

"I want to see you," she said. Then she got up and sat astride me on the window ledge.

I reached up to clear the hair from her face, but she caught my thumb between her teeth. As she took me in her hand, I tried to adjust myself so that we were leaning against the wall, rather than the glass, but then she was rolling a condom on and guiding me inside her. We were ten stories above the city. She rocked against me, and I imagined the window breaking, the two of us exploding out into the night in a starry burst of sweat and glass. Instead she came, and I whispered, *Hold on to me.*

She did, and I carried her to the bed. She was still gasping. I reached under her and tilted her hips toward mine, driving into her with all of my weight. When she came again, I heard myself shout.

"What's your name?" she said, once I opened my eyes.

She was facing me, still flushed, a wisp of darkened hair clinging to her temple. I brushed it back.

"I mean it." She stifled a laugh. "That's the best sex I've ever had, and I don't remember your name."

WE SAW EACH OTHER whenever we could that next year. She had recently left her long-term boyfriend—he realized he wanted children; she didn't—and was wary of starting another relationship too soon. I was still shuttling between job interviews. When she won a Fulbright to study the Bornean green magpie, which would take her to Malaysia until the following summer, I was sure our days were numbered. But we kept talking. The less practical our reunions became, the more inevitable they felt. Once I landed a full-time job at the College—and the tripled salary it promised—I flew out three times to see her. We met in Phnom Penh, then Kyoto. We spent Christmas in Bangkok. I was smitten by then, and tormented with longing. During my spring vacation, I rented us a cottage on the eastern shore of Cape Cod. It was there that she first said she loved me.

I could have wept or screamed. Instead I said it back, and held her, and felt my torment lessen subtly, in the way a diagnosis can relieve a foreign ache—not by altering the pain, but by deciphering it.

She had grown up in a small coastal town in Connecticut, where her mother, Nadia—the child of Holocaust survivors— taught at a Jewish day school. Frank, a college dropout and autodidact, handled accounting for their local bookstore. His career had been something of a suicide mission, she said. The child of

Polish immigrants, he had initially worked as a union orga-
nizer, salting construction firms. After three failed campaigns,
he picked up a string of blue-collar jobs in which, as far as Prue
could tell, he had taken stubborn pleasure. He even seemed to
relish being fired. At the bookstore that finally hired him, he
was demoted twice for reclassifying books at whim. (*The Feder-
alist Papers* represented one of the many volumes he exported
from History to Religion, a category he later rebranded Self-
Help.) His antics exasperated Prue's mother, but only in princi-
ple. Between her salary and a modest inheritance from Frank's
late father, Prue explained, the family had little need for a second
income.

"He's only medicated thanks to my mom," she said.

We had spread a blanket on the beach, and were sharing a
picnic of roast beef and ciabatta. The bloodied paper lay between
us, canting in the breeze, pinned in place by a bottle of Malbec.
The sea was quiet. We were more or less alone. Besides Prue's
voice, the only sound was the hiss of marram grass, planted years
ago to stabilize the dunes.

"Since she died, he's been skimping on his pills." She refilled
my Dixie cup with wine. "I can usually tell when he's off them.
Not always, though."

The breeze picked up, carrying salt. We had showered before
lunch, and her hair—swept back into a braid—was still damp.
Golden wisps flickered at her temple.

As I draped my coat around her shoulders she turned. "Do
you really want to hear this?"

She looked at me. The light, cool though it was, had planted
a ripening burn on her cheeks.

"Of course." I fished for the sunscreen. I had yet to meet her family, but she had promised to introduce me soon. "I want to hear everything about you."

"Okay," she said, exhaling. Then she gave a doleful laugh. "It's almost funny, it's so bizarre."

I dabbed the sunscreen on her face as she began: "I was eight at the time. My mom drove me home from Hebrew school, dead of winter, and he was gone. Walt"—a toddler at the time—"was wandering through the house, crying. My mom called the bookstore, the library, all Dad's friends. Nothing. That he could have abandoned Walt was just unthinkable—he was a helicopter parent before it was fashionable—so we were totally at a loss." She scratched the corner of her mouth and took a breath. "My mom starts saying that everything will be fine, which is when I get scared. It gets dark. She calls the cops. I'm entertaining Walt, trying to hold it together. The heater's blasting, so the windows are fogged over, and we're doodling on the one facing the yard. At one point Walt presses his nose against the pane, then spazzes out—laughing, flapping his hands. I try it too, for kicks. That's when I see him."

"Your father?"

Although a cloud had come over the sun, she was still squinting as she added, "He was outside, naked, staring at me."

"Jesus," I said.

She dug her toes into the sand. "I don't remember much after that. I know I screamed, and Walt started bawling. My mom sent the two of us upstairs before she dragged him inside, but I could still hear him through the floor. He kept shouting at her, even after the cops showed up, that he'd discovered the truth about the universe." She smiled unconvincingly. "New Age crap."

I took her hand. "That's so frightening."

"Yeah." She withdrew her hand and ripped off another wedge of ciabatta, which she did not eat. "It was a one-time deal, though. The doctors got him on Depakote and it never happened again. They called it late-onset bipolar, which he never bought, even though he promised my mom he'd stay medicated. The thing is . . . " She folded a layer of roast beef over the bread. "He kind of changed, after that. He started watching TV, which he used to hate. He stopped telling as many stories."

She blew a fly off my shoulder and took a bite, gazing out at the corrugated sea. A small sailboat had coasted into view, steered by a lone figure. The boat was tacking, the sail rippling and then wagging comically as the figure scrambled to rein in the boom.

"He'd had this whole repertoire," Prue went on. "Like, every time Walt or I lost a tooth we would bury it in the yard. He said it would grow into a tree with moons on the branches." She laughed. "The tooth fairy really pissed him off. He had this spiel about exchanging body parts for cash. A Faustian bargain, in his mind."

"And he stopped doing all that, after the diagnosis?" I said, guiding her back to the thread of our conversation. Across the sand, a bird pecked at the shadow of a wave.

"Not entirely." She stretched, her voice warped by a yawn. "But yeah, for the most part. And it kind of poisoned my memories of him, because it meant his old self was actually sick. So I felt horribly guilty for missing it."

I kissed her shoulder as she added, "He did the craziest shit when I was little. There was this time he drove us to the town landfill. We spent two hours wading through trash. His idea was to gather materials for a gramophone small enough to play our fingerprints."

"Thrilling your mother, I'm sure."

As she laughed, I wondered whether it was the contrast I posed to her father that had attracted her to me. It seemed possible that his turbulence could solve the puzzle that still haunted me occasionally: how a beautiful, gifted person with the world at her feet could have settled for a fusty scholar with three papers to his name.

To dispel the thought I asked, "Does that old version ever reappear, when he's off his meds?"

"Not really." She hesitated. "Or maybe I just don't find it magical anymore."

A gull swerved toward us, wailed its high flat note. I glanced ahead, past the sailboat, looking for the stroke that distinguished the sky from the glittering surf. But there was fog in the distance, and all I made out were gradations of blue.

WHEN PRUE FINISHED her Fulbright she moved in with me, and we eloped the following spring. That summer—six years ago, come June—we moved into our apartment on the bottom floor of an old Victorian house near campus. Her career took off after that. The College hired her immediately as a lecturer in biology, then as an assistant professor. By her third year she had even marshaled funds for the new Center for Ornithology: the

first of its kind at a liberal arts college. She still teaches her pop-
ular seminar in evolutionary psychology, while I lecture in epistemology and introductory logic. My monograph on the Gettier
problem—finally finished after more than ten years—has been
turned down by all but one of the major academic publishers, but
I have hope for the smaller houses.

We are happy, as far as I can tell. Still passionate. Comfortable, especially in light of my recent (and her imminent) promo-
tion. Lately, though, I have had the impression of a rift. The
signs—dropped glances, rushed embraces, abbreviated meals—
are so subtle I have probably imagined them. Nonetheless, I can't
shake the sense that we are living in a minor key. "Has something changed?" I want to say, and almost have. But each time I
formulate the question in my mind, she preempts it with a warm
look, or laugh, and my fears seem asinine.

I wish we would fight to clear the air. We almost did just
yesterday, when we had some colleagues over for drinks after a
faculty meeting. Prue proposed the gathering spontaneously, as a
group of us were leaving the hall, so I had no choice but to parrot
her invitation. I would much rather have gone home to work.

Although it was supposed to snow on Friday, the weather was
ludicrously warm—in the high fifties—so we pulled some chairs
around our glass table out back. There were six of us: Prue and
me; Adaora Ironsi, an economist and close friend of Prue's; her
husband, Edson Gerlach, a chaired professor of neuroscience;
Quinn Bates, an anthropologist; and a new faculty member we
hadn't met before, who knew Edson from graduate school. "That's
Dalton Field," Quinn whispered to me as we walked over from

campus. He was a prominent novelist, apparently, though I had never heard of him. Unlike Prue I don't read much fiction.

"Back in the eighties, the point was to offend," Dalton was saying now, as we sat around the table. "This generation finds it sexier to get offended."

He helped himself to more of our Chablis. He was a tall man, black, and garishly handsome, dressed in a gray cashmere sweater and Italian wingtips. There was a fat gold band on his wedding finger. Nonetheless, when Quinn stood up he glanced at her ass.

"Were you even alive in the eighties?" Adaora said, as I pointed Quinn toward our bathroom. Wind rattled the dry leaves overhead.

"Come on, Daora." He spread his arms, incredulous. "The left has sold its soul to political correctness."

While I happened to agree, I disliked him already. It was unseemly, this readiness to hold court on our turf. His tone smacked of that complacent breed of pessimism I had indulged back in my twenties. *The world is rotten,* it went in my case, *so even those who move through it gracefully are suspect. Everyone, that is, but me.*

I tried to catch Prue's eye but she was smirking at him. She said, "Something you'd like to share?"

She was conscious of being beautiful, of the special power that came from being both beautiful and smart, and of how to exercise that power in conversation. The more incisive her contributions, she once remarked, in a rare display of cynicism, the more likely they were to elicit from her male interlocutor a bashful deference, disguised as respect. He would nod, even toast her point, all in order to conceal his surprise that the two—intelligence and beauty—could intersect. Men like Dalton were the ones I'd thought she'd had in mind.

"Nothing kosher, I'm afraid," he said, holding her gaze as she plucked the second-to-last truffle from the case I had set out.

Adaora glanced at me. When I caught her eye, her mouth sprang into a smile.

I said, "I wouldn't say Phil Barker speaks for liberal America."

Before Dalton's segue, Adaora had been complaining about Barker—the new dean—who had announced a mandatory training module in "inclusion and professional respect" at the faculty meeting. It seemed reasonable to me, given the recent harassment allegations by a postdoc in psychology, though I resented the bureaucratese.

"He's not saying that," Prue said, so dismissively that Edson—who had been murmuring something to Adaora—fell silent. "The point is, if you try to say anything new these days, you become a persona non grata."

"Case in point." I raised my hands, and Edson laughed.

Dalton was watching her too now, steadily. Could they have met before? Impossible—Adaora had just introduced them today. But their silence had a covert, inward quality, sure as a fever hatching in the bones.

"Prue, can you tell me where you keep the tea?" Quinn called, leaning through the back door.

"You sit." I stood up. "I'll take care of it."

"Anything herbal would be great," she said, as she brushed past me. She was going through a divorce from her husband of eight years, but she looked lovely as ever. Her dark eyes glowed with intelligence, and though she was my age—no older than fifty, surely—her curls were white.

I filled the kettle and watched the five of them through the window, pocked with bird shit and dried rain. Washing it—yet another chore to keep me from my desk. *Just accept it,* I thought grimly. *You will never publish again.*

The conversation had splintered in two: Quinn, Adaora, and Edson chatting lazily across the table, and Dalton opining to Prue. When he finished she leaned forward, whispering something that prompted him to cover his mouth in astonishment. She laughed, and so did he, and then he composed himself and began speaking again, magnifying her expression with his own, until his story ended and they stared at each other in mock surprise before dissolving again in laughter.

"What did I miss?" I said, emerging onto the patio with Quinn's chamomile tea.

"I was just saying I would put Prue in touch with our friends in Heidelberg," Adaora replied. As Quinn leaned across the table for a meringue, Adaora murmured: "Honey, you've got something. . . ." Quinn glanced at the back of her skirt, cursed, and then rubbed at a tiny smear of chocolate.

"I'll be in Munich in April, come to think of it," Dalton said.

"When I was there—" Quinn began, and then broke off as Dalton muttered something to Edson, who chortled.

I faced Quinn to show her I was listening, but she said nothing, still waiting for their attention.

"You'll love it," Edson said to Prue. He was a shy man with kind eyes and a small, doughy face. I still hadn't read the paper that had earned him the coveted Gruber Prize in neuroscience earlier this year, though Prue had. Something to do with Alzheimer's.

Lifting his wineglass, he added, "The Institute's close to the city, as I remember."

Prue glanced at me uneasily, and I realized what he was referring to: the Max Planck Institute for Ornithology, whose directors had offered her a half-year research appointment starting in January. A high honor, certainly, but with her tenure review coming up next semester it made no practical sense.

"She already turned it down," I said, refilling my glass.

There was a silence, and then Prue cleared her throat. "Actually, I haven't yet."

"Are you joking?" I searched her face for irony. Trying to sound casual, I added, "What about your review?"

"I don't think she has anything to worry about," Adaora said.

Heat crept into my cheeks. If she was still considering a stint abroad, I should have been the first to hear about it. I shot her a look that said as much, but was squinting at the sky.

"You scholars with your golden handcuffs," Dalton said. He rotated his glass on its stem. "I'd say, go for it. Somewhere in time, you're dead."

There was a round of hollow laughter. Then the conversation drifted on.

"What was that about, before?" I said, when they had finally left us to ourselves. Prue didn't answer. She started carrying in another chair, but I stepped in her way.

"What?" she demanded.

"The Germany thing."

From overhead came the sound of arpeggios, faint at first, and then louder. The pianist upstairs—a slim, reluctant man—was warming up.

She set down the chair and sighed. It had rained that morning, and in the washed afternoon light her hair looked reddish gold.

"I don't get it," I said. "You're up for tenure."

"You keep saying that, as though it would hurt my case. I actually think—"

"To request a leave of absence *now*?" I interrupted. When she narrowed her eyes, I added, "They'd probably push your review back another year, at least."

"Would that be the end of the world?"

The wind blew her dress against her thighs. Her nonchalance about something I had worked so hard for, something so self-evidently desirable—insurance on the life we had made here, no less—had been surfacing more and more frequently.

I tried another angle. "It just doesn't seem like the right time, P."

"It's never the right time, is it?"

She shot me the same reproachful look she had last month, after I nixed her idea of applying to the Rome Prize together. *It would be like when we were dating,* she had said. *Don't you miss traveling together?* Her feigned naïveté had made me even angrier. It wasn't as though I would have had a shot.

"For god's sake," I said, goaded by the thought of how sheepish she would be when I surprised her this weekend with the

Galápagos tickets. "Give the jet-setting a rest. You're almost tenured."

In silence, she carried the chair into the house. I twirled the empty wine bottle in my hands, read the label, and then set it back down.

The door opened again, and she returned with a sponge. To my surprise, she said, "You're right."

I waited for her to elaborate, but all she did was cross the patio and wipe down the table.

"I didn't realize you were still considering it," I said.

She tossed a shard of meringue into the bushes.

I added, "To bring it up in front of everyone—that guy we barely know . . ."

"I get it. I fucked up."

"If you want to leave for a semester, fine, but at least—"

"I just said I wouldn't go."

She was blinking fiercely. The pianist had moved on to scales: major, ascending. At each octave he lingered, with obscene feeling, on the seventh key.

"I'm an asshole, is that it?" I said. When she did not reply, I concluded, "I'm an asshole."

She laughed softly. I moved behind her and laced my arms under hers, burying my face in her hair.

"I'm sorry," I said. "If you want to go, go, I'd just—"

"No." She shook her head. "You have a point—it's not strategic."

"I'd miss you."

As she detached herself I gestured at the fiery clouds.

"It's still beautiful," I said.

"Yeah."

"A walk would be nice."

It was an invitation, but she only smiled absently.

"Come back soon," she said.

I nodded.

"I'll heat up some food."

She kissed me nearer to the corner of my lips than the center. Then she turned and went into the house.

Three

———

How the hell'd he not know about your article?" Frank asks, as I follow the two of them into the kitchen. The light is low, the heat on high, trapping the sweet, resinous odor of whatever she cooked for dinner.

"Am I a journalist now?" Prue tosses her windbreaker over a stool and rubs her bare shoulders. She has Frank's square jaw, his freckles. It always unnerves me, mildly, to see him reflected in her.

"He means the shout-out in the *Times*," I say.

"Oh . . ." She wrinkles her nose. "That was weeks ago."

Frank drags out a stool and perches at the counter, not bothering to take off his coat. "Don't play it down, pumpkin." He cracks the knuckle of his middle finger against his jaw. "This is big."

"You feeling okay, Dad?" Prue says. To me she murmurs, "How was the drive?"

"We hit some traffic on 95." I drop my keys on the windowsill. "Smooth, other—"

"Never been better." Frank slaps the counter. "You renovate? Place is looking good."

"No," Prue says. She opens the dishwasher, releasing a gush of steam. "I would have told you that."

From the upper tray she removes a glass and dries it against her shirt—the beige tank top she usually sleeps in, streaked with burns from the dryer we have since replaced. There are shadows under her eyes.

I am about to offer to show Frank into the guest room when her phone chimes with a text. Peering down at it she says, "Walt wants to leave May with us overnight, tomorrow."

"So she can spend more time with you," I tell Frank.

And he can have Julia over, Prue does not add. She shoots me a warm look. After three painful years, he is finally seeing someone new.

Frank seizes her phone. "See how the world has migrated since the hieroglyphs?" he says. "Stone to trees to light."

We stare at him. The furnace clicks. He addresses us with a ferocity—exultant, somehow comic—that I have encountered in no other human face.

"*Words,*" he adds. "The home of words. First in caves, then on paper, now in light."

"I'm going to need that back, Dad," Prue says slowly.

He brandishes the phone, which trembles in his hand. To my surprise, I find myself intrigued, relieved by her impatience of having to play the sensible one.

"Holiest of elements," Frank says. "Question is, where do they go from here? Nowhere"—he tosses the phone onto the counter—"nowhere left."

Prue pockets it and strides back to the dishwasher, yanking out the bottom tray. As she unloads the utensils, the color rising in her neck, I feel an unexpected flare of irritation. *If this is too much for you,* I think ungenerously, *try sharing a car with him for three and a half hours.*

To repent, I lift Frank's bag. "Why don't we get you set up?" I say. But he ignores me.

"For most of time, machines were breaking laws," he says. "Rockets to flout gravity, trains and telephones to conquer space. Then they stopped defying God and started playing Him."

Prue slides a stack of plates into the cupboard and turns, wiping her palms on the rear of her leggings.

Meeting her gaze, Frank throws out his arms. "We're remaking the world in our little light boxes, and destroying the earth in the process."

"Sounds like you've been reading your Kant," I say, but he only cracks another knuckle, his eyes sparkling.

"Come on, Dad," Prue says, taking his duffel from my hand. "It's getting late."

Frank salutes me, then follows her into the corridor. As they disappear their voices come to me as music, stripped of consonants: Prue's calm, declarative; Frank's adrenalized. I take a breath. In three days, she will be driving him home. We will be back to our usual rhythms.

Chirping filters from the study: our cockatiel, Rex, my gift to Prue on our first anniversary. Pushing open the door, I find that she has forgotten to feed him, so I shake a bag of pellets over his plastic trough, fighting his attempts to clamber up my arm.

Prue claimed the study initially, but after she opened her lab at the College—and the second office it afforded her—we decided I should take it. I prefer the room to my glorified cubby in the Philosophy building, where students come knocking outside my office hours, and whose walls are so thin that my colleagues can practically hear me think.

I close the cage before Rex can escape, accidentally trapping his wing.

"Shit." I open and shut it again. "Sorry, buddy."

He lurches back, beak parted, and clicks his tongue. Then he attacks the pellets, his yellow plume bobbing as he eats.

I had meant to give my monograph a final read tonight, before submitting it tomorrow to Cornell University Press. My half sabbatical has left my schedule emptier than usual—I am teaching one course, logic, rather than my standard two—but the easing of one burden has magnified the rest. The paradox is familiar: the more time I have, the more daunting my lessened obligations seem, suffusing my weekdays like a gas.

But there is a chapter by my undergraduate logic TA, Natasha Díaz—a double major in philosophy and biology—that I have promised to return tomorrow. It is finely written, so far, if overambitious: a Wittgensteinian critique of the quest for an "ideal language" that animated early analytic philosophy. The concept electrified me when I first encountered it in graduate school: a language comprised exclusively of factual statements and logical propositions, capable of representing the world with perfect accuracy. Like the symbols of mathematics, the words of this language would accommodate no ambiguity. Within it, philosophical problems would vanish, because they could no longer be articulated. There would be no controversy over definitions, no margin between what was meant and what was said. The purpose of philosophy, as the early analytic school saw it, was to distill ordinary language, into this ideal language eliminating misunderstandings once and for all.

Perhaps out of sympathy for that beautiful—albeit doomed—endeavor, I have never been drawn to Wittgenstein's work, and have made my reservations clear to Natasha. Nonetheless, she requested me as her spring advisor, and with our resident philosopher of language on leave, I agreed to play the part.

Rex starts flapping madly—a habit of his—a sound like the shuffling of cards. He does it to exercise his wings, Prue explained to me once, even though we give him free rein of the apartment during the day. When I bought him, I thought it might bother her to lock him up at all, until I remembered that she spent her days with captive birds. The aviary she helped design at the College's Center for Ornithology bears no resemblance to a cage, however. With its acre of outdoor land and lush, glassed-in indoor wing, it rivals the enclosures at major research universities. *"The bird McMansion,"* I call it. The alumnus who underwrote the project—a former veterinary surgeon—enjoys full access, much to Prue's irritation. I think the privilege is the least he deserves, given what he shelled out.

The flapping intensifies, punctuated by a trill. Rex's noises usually soothe me, but tonight they shatter my focus. After reading the same paragraph twice, I give up and face the window, massaging my temples. My reflection stares back, looking older than it should.

Giving up, I switch off the lamp and move into the hallway. The light is still on in the kitchen; Prue must be snacking or reading. Relieved at the thought of having the bedroom to myself, I push open the door, and nearly jump to find her standing at the bureau.

"He's bad," she says.

She is braiding her hair, which she has blow-dried. Steam wends from the mug before her.

"You heard him in there." She meets my eye in the mirror. "He's talking like he's a fucking prophet."

I lift her mug to check for a stain on the dresser—none, thankfully—and slide a copy of her alumni bulletin from Pomona underneath it. She must have been in here for a while, because a hardcover is splayed across her pillow.

"You're sure he took it?" she says.

I nod, wrapping my arms around her. As she tips her head against my chest I picture Frank in the diner's parking lot, downing the pill in the frosty cabin. The scene carries the force of a memory. Why shouldn't I take him at his word? And even if he had been lying, one pill can't make much difference.

"He's going to pull something during my speech," she says. "I can feel it."

She speaks as though he has some power over her. *Can't you see how diminished he is?* I want to say. *He's a batty old man, P. Practically broke. Soon he'll be beholden to you and Walt.*

My own mother saved so assiduously that I never spent a penny on her care. When her dementia worsened, I moved her into a nursing home outside of Boston, where I had returned after finishing my PhD. Glaucoma had narrowed her visual field to a single point of light, the doctors said, which I would occupy, briefly, leaning down to kiss her. I probably registered only as a shadow. So much the better that she couldn't see the fluttering room dividers, I reasoned, the mounted televisions spouting infomercials, the beige of her corn bread, and every other anodyne assault on personality in that place. I would sit in the faux leather chair beside her bed, reading aloud from her battered copy of Tennyson's *In Memoriam*, often in counterpoint to the voice of her roommate, a former news anchor, who joked and nattered long into the night. After a few months her pupils clouded and her murmured greetings stopped. It still disturbs me how, if my sense of duty toward her signaled nothing but abiding love, her death could have carried such relief.

"How was he in the car?" Prue says.

"Effusive, the usual."

She takes a premature sip of tea, flinches, and then toys with my wedding band. At some point over the past few years, she developed an allergy to the nickel in hers, grafted to the silver plate to help forestall corrosion. I keep meaning to surprise her with a bronze version like mine, but I have yet to get around to it.

"He's a proud dad." I disengage and unbutton my shirt. "Why didn't you tell me about the *Times* piece?"

"Thought I did." She glances at the painting above the bed: a lake at evening—half of it frozen, the other half scalloped by wind. "I'll send it to you if you want," she adds. "It was nothing huge."

From the tone of her voice—suddenly flip—and the deepening color in her cheeks, I can tell that her modesty is insincere. She is understated in general, especially about her work, but she has been conspicuously tactful lately. This most recent study marks her twentieth published article—albeit as a coauthor—to my four. I lob my shirt into the hamper, trying to catch her eye. Though she is only trying to spare my pride, I can't help but feel that she is pandering.

"Frank seems to think it was a national headline," I say, more sarcastically than I've intended.

"See?" She props her left leg on the bed, pumping a coil of lotion onto her palm. "He's manic."

"He's excited for you."

"I know you don't take him seriously, but I'm worried about the lecture, what he might—"

"What's he going to do, shout profanities? He's a passionate old man, P, not a maniac."

"Fine." She tosses her free hand. "Let him interrupt me, if he wants. Keep things interesting."

In swift, irregular strokes, she works the lotion into her thigh. It strikes me, as it has before, how recklessly she handles her body; how it seems to mean more to me than it does to her.

"I doubt anyone will show up, anyway," she mutters. "They're saying we're supposed to get three inches of snow."

"Are you planning to gloss the birdsong study?" I say, softening.

"Are you interested?"

A question, an indictment. She has a point. As she stares at me defiantly—or is it hungrily?—a line from the Chomsky biography comes to mind: *Animals can no more talk than Olympian high jumpers can fly.*

"Of course I'm interested." I move toward her. "You'll have tenure in the bag after this."

She snickers and steps out of her underwear, wiping the remains of the lotion on her hips. Then she pulls me against her.

"Listen." I press my lips to her forehead. "Let me handle things tomorrow. The day after next I promised May I'd take her to the aquarium. Frank can come with us. You can get some . . ."

The book on her pillow is that man's. As she tugs off my belt I register the precious title—*Forgive Me Not*—dwarfed by his name: Dalton Field.

"You bought his novel," I hear myself say.

"Hmm?" She has moved on to my zipper.

"That guy from yesterday—the writer."

"Yeah, why?"

"He seemed like a hack."

She laughs. "Stay angry, I like it."

"Really." I step back, no longer in the mood, and her face clouds. "Sorry, I just . . ." I scratch my neck.

"What's your problem?" she says.

"I've been on the road all day, P. I'm tired."

I turn toward the bathroom, hating the sound of my own voice. I had offered to drive Frank, after all, and have no business whining about it.

"Fine." She slides under the quilt. "I owe you for today."

"You don't owe me anything," I say miserably, as she picks up *Forgive Me Not.* "I'm going to shower."

Without looking at me, she nods, already settling back into the book.

Instead I undress and climb into the tub, letting the thundering water creep over my shins, and then my thighs. The usual wreckage drifts toward me—unanswered emails, neglected tasks—synecdoche for the mounting impression that I am doing life wrong, or living the wrong life. *Posttenure blues,* I remind myself. To scare them off I lean over the rim to dry my hands on my khakis, then pull my phone out of the back pocket to check the news. Today's headlines only depress me further.

Already dizzy from the heat, I set the phone down and lather my face. By the time I have wrenched myself out of the water, the strip of lamplight under the bathroom door is gone.

Prue is still asleep when I crawl in beside her. She is breathing lightly, her back to me, but when I slip my arm under her bicep she doesn't stir. Her breasts are heavy and warm. I nudge my face into her hair, and hear a soft, plosive sound as her lips separate. Then I thread my hand between her thighs.

She doesn't mind being touched in sleep. The first time I did it, I woke her up to confess. She laughed and said she liked the idea. She had probably done the same to me. Her amusement chastened me, but didn't spoil my excitement. There was something exquisitely strange about encountering her there in her own absence. When she is awake the touch is a disclosure, an invitation. But now it means what it is, and nothing else.

"I love you," I whisper.

She shifts. As I free my hand a phrase leaves her—garbled, beseeching—addressed to some dreamed interlocutor.

Four

———

I wake up to banging. It is still dark, but a bluish light is leaking through the ribs of the venetian blinds. When I switch on the lamp, Prue only groans and burrows deeper under the quilt. My phone reads 6:03. The banging intensifies. Cursing, I roll out of bed and into my bathrobe, but no sooner have I left the room than the house goes quiet. I pause in the threshold, wondering whether I have imagined the disturbance. Then another sound comes, too faint to decipher. At once the banging resumes, accelerated, in low, staccato thumps.

I edge into the corridor, careful to avoid the loose floorboards that would broadcast my approach. The door of the utility closet has been flung open, its hanging bulb flickering. The noise is coming from the living room. Through its glass doors I see only blackness, until my eyes adjust to a figure brandishing a tall dark rod. Instead of swinging it he is thrusting it upward, hitting the ceiling, the room quaking with each thump. Frank. Of course.

I fling open the door, switching on the overhead light, and he squints toward me, broom in hand.

"Do you have a *tenant*?" he says.

"What the hell are you doing?"

"I thought you owned this place."

"It's a duplex, Frank."

A piano chord sounds overhead, tentative. Before I can stop him he is at it again, so I lunge forward and wrench the broom away from him.

"Who plays scales at six a.m.?" He opens his arms. "Dvořák, okay, but *scales?*"

By the time I have cajoled him back to bed I am hopelessly awake, and famished. Prue has finished all the bacon. I resort to a toasted bagel with cream cheese, eating over the sink to watch the sunrise. The stars have receded, leaving a chilly, lunar glow. The bagel has slaked my hunger, but not that different grade of hankering—for catatonia, oblivion—that usually goads me into a binge.

Nine days since my last. I do my best to space them out. When enough time passes—two weeks, say—I delude myself that I have kicked the habit. Almost as soon as the thought occurs to me, the hankering rears up again, as if on cue, and makes a mockery of my resolve. *Fuck it,* I think, and stuff the last of the bagel in my mouth, compensating with the thought of a trip to the gym before class.

The fridge is ripe with options, including Prue's Terra chips—open, fortunately—five meringues left over from Wednesday, and the small red cheese wheels we keep around for May. I start with the chips, forcing myself to leave a good handful, and then yield to the cheese. After demolishing two wheels, I raid the stash of soppressata we save for guests, finally close to the zenith—the sense of plenitude that washes over me before disgust sets in. While I would never admit it, I prefer the feeling to sex. It is the closest I have felt to transcendence: standing here on the linoleum before the spoils of our lives, sating the thing that's reaching through me, into the cool white light.

In the freezer I locate my habitual finale: chocolate sorbet. I hold the carton under steaming water, and am closing my mouth around the first ambrosial bite when someone speaks.

"Save some for me, kid."

I nearly choke. Coughing, I shrink away from Frank, but he reaches out and pounds my back.

"Needed to ask," he says. "Do you have a camcorder by any chance?"

I switch on the overhead light—anything to gain some distance from him—and find that he has changed out of his nightclothes. The same plaid shirt he wore yesterday hangs from his frame, half of it stuffed into his boxers.

"We use our phones." My face burns. "Why?"

"Prue's speech—"

"The College tapes it."

The taste of sausage lingers in my mouth, revolting me. I turn to stow the sorbet carton in the freezer, but he catches my forearm.

"I'm serious."

"I told you, they—"

"That." He gestures at the pint. "Can I have a little?"

"It's dawn, Frank."

"Didn't stop you."

As he wolfs down his scoop he roams the dining area, pausing now and then to inspect the books—most of them Prue's—that litter the table and chairs. I boil myself a cup of ginger tea, trying to conjure some semblance of poise.

"Cordelia loves this crap," he says.

His cat, he means—a tabby he coaxed out of a drainpipe late last year. I dip a spoon in my tea to cool it, counting to ten to settle my nerves.

"Landlord wants me to chuck her," Frank adds. "Man's a born-again, and he's evicting her in Christmas season, of all times."

"It's his house," I can't resist replying. "His terms."

"Hey." Frank jabs the air with his spoon. A drop of chocolate sails from the tip onto Prue's windbreaker, still prostrate over the stool. "Prue said you finished your book?"

She has proofread countless drafts of my monograph, and comforted me when the first rejections trickled in. I have yet to tell her about the latest, from Routledge.

"Says it's not too shabby." Frank watches me tear off a segment of paper towel and run it under hot water. As I dab the spot on her windbreaker he adds, "About the relation between data and knowledge, or something? How the one's never a sufficient condition for the other?"

"I should pay you to pitch it at conferences," I say.

"*Conferences.*" He chuckles, loading his dirty bowl into the dishwasher. "So that's what philosophers do."

As he retreats into the corridor I feel the cold, damp wind of this contempt, and realize I have had enough.

"You know what, Frank?"

He turns.

"You can shut your goddamn mouth."

Delight, mingled with sadness, crosses his face. He waits in silence, and to my chagrin only seems to brighten when I add, "It might come as a surprise to you, but I don't happen to care what you think of my life."

We stare at each other. The only sound is the refrigerator's hum.

At last he says, "That's what I like to see."

"What are you—"

"Rage."

"For Christ's sake . . . " I sidestep him and angle toward the study, forgetting my tea.

"Follow it," he calls. "Or it'll keep on chasing you."

Shutting the door I stand for a moment in darkness. Gradually the shapes announce themselves: the lamp, the couch, the hump of Rex's cage.

As a child, shunted awake by a nightmare, I trained myself to slip from bed and stand like this in the center of my room, the point from which I could regard each of my toys. Armed with shadows, the silhouettes of my tin soldiers and Tonka trucks petrified me, but I forced myself to face them down. In a low voice, almost a whisper, I would repeat their names. Night had stripped each object of a kind of cage, or embankment, I felt—whatever boundary ensured that it remained itself. The boundary kept the object from becoming something else, something hysterical or mad, and my naming restored it, somehow. The ritual haunted me well into my preteen years, though I managed to keep it from my mother. An early flare of OCD, perhaps.

I turn on the lamp. On my desk is a paper I have agreed to

review for the *Journal of Symbolic Logic.* "On Algebraic Closure in Pseudofinite Fields," reads the title. I turn the page. "ABSTRACT: We present the automorphism group of the algebraic closure of a substructure A of a pseudo-finite field F. We show that the behavior of this group, even when A is large, depends on its roots of unity in $F \ldots$ "

I let the page fall and open my laptop. Into Google I type "Dalton Field."

The results number in the tens of thousands. Most of them are reviews of *Forgive Me Not,* his third novel, which has been called "searing" by *Esquire.* The sidebar features several head shots, some black and white, and all of them heavy on the contrast. It also reveals that he is thirty-nine years old, a Princeton graduate, and married to someone named Robin Rothschild.

It figures; he has the look of money, and as a writer he can't have made much of it himself. The images page shows him at various galas, his arms thrown around women, while the first video result depicts a commencement address he apparently delivered this year at Haverford College. I click on it.

"Congratulations," he booms, tassel swinging. I skip ahead, lowering the volume.

". . . fear and heartache . . ."

I skip again.

". . . what a novelist actually does all day . . ."

Once more.

"Here is life: I shave. I shit. I run the bathwater so hot that the steam empties the mirror. I check the forecast, forget the figure, read the newspaper so I can complain more knowledgeably. Meanwhile, offstage, all that news is converted into History—

plausible, suddenly, because it was the road that led to now. Dictators fall. The landlord dyes his hair. It is an effort not to live as if asleep—trusting myself to dress and eat, chat with my friends, run errands. Months pass that way, and then in flashes I am back—watching the velvet seats reappear after a movie, sneezing, hacking the ice off my car. I find myself in restaurants, sometimes joyful, more often numb, telling the difference by whether or not I've noticed the breeze on my skin, the applauding leaves, the housefly cleaning its face. Wondering, throughout, whose life I'm walking through. Disliking the person I love."

I can't help but smile. What had he been thinking, subjecting thousands of strangers to his poetized weltschmerz? It's not that the man seems boastful, exactly. But he radiates a familiar, masculine impatience, the bravado of the spiritually passive. It seems important to him that—out of envy or awe—his listeners will come away from the talk having failed to grasp his point.

He pauses for effect, his eyes laughing. "Not so, in literature," he is saying now. "Literature, assuming it's any good, conforms to a shape that human lives don't actually *assume*." The Sophoclean dramas, the bildungsroman, what have you. They are compelling because they endow the lives of their heroes with a pattern—comic, tragic, ironic—and for that reason they are also cruel. How can you read them without suspecting that your own life is flawed, anemic? That you are to blame for the fact that the plot you've undertaken has no climax and would not, therefore, make for a particularly absorbing read?"

I stop the video, sliding the cursor over the button shaped like a downward thumb. A strip of text appears: "I dislike this." Click. The tally of "dislikes" rises to 7, beside the 302 "likes." Ashamed, I close the laptop.

ONLY THREE-QUARTERS of my students show up for my logic class later that day, probably thanks to the impending snow. A few come late, missing the exam review sheet I handed out at the beginning.

"Julius Caesar had twenty-six teeth at the time of his death," I say. "True or false?"

They stare at me blankly, probably thinking of food or sex. The question is rhetorical, to be fair. Having finished my lecture early, I am killing the last few minutes with a thought experiment.

"According to the verifiability criterion, that question should be nonsense," I continue. "It can't possibly be confirmed or denied now that the evidence is gone. And yet . . ." I lean against the blackboard, tossing my nub of chalk from one hand to the other. "Intuition tells us that it has an answer."

My stomach churns. Between editing Natasha's chapter and rereading my monograph one last time before submitting a proposal and excerpt to the editor at Cornell, I hadn't made time for a workout after all.

"It *is* nonsense, to some people," a boy named Jacob calls out.

He is one of my problem students—*your gadfly,* Prue calls him, although she knows him only through my complaints.

Initially, I worried he would derail the class, but the other students quickly turned against him. Now he rarely pipes up.

"Like that tribe in the Amazon," Jacob adds, "who don't have numbers, only words for 'one' and 'many.'"

There is a general shuffling.

"Even if that's true," I say, "it happens not to matter for our purposes."

A few students click their pens closed, a signal that class has ended, even though we still have three minutes left.

"But those people wouldn't make head or tail of a sentence like that," he persists. He rakes his fingers through his greasy blond hair. "Any more than we would make much sense of the fifty Inuit words for snow."

So he is still impressed by relativism, cultural chauvinism's latest guise. Before I can shoot him down Natasha comes to my rescue.

"Save it for section, Jacob," she says, from her perch at the end of the second row. As she smiles at me knowingly, winding her ankle, a few students laugh.

"Natasha!" I call, as they stream out.

She turns, surprised, and I wave her thesis chapter in the air. As she strolls toward me, a group of stragglers—Jacob among them—sidle up for the review sheet.

"I'm heading to Mudd, by the way," she says over their heads. In a short skirt and tights, she is underdressed for the cold. She takes the chapter, her painted nail grazing my thumb.

Her voice, with its clipped vowels, has always reminded me of Madeleine's. She is not Swedish, however, but Mexican, the child—I learned after Googling her, idly, late one night—of a coal magnate. That she has taken the liberty of addressing me as "Ivan" in her emails, ever since I became her advisor, should irritate me. But the shyness in her huge brown eyes, combined with her eagerness to please, has stopped me from correcting her.

Registering my confusion, she says, "To see Professor Baum?"

"Yes, of course." Prue, she means. I have to get over there, in fact—the lecture is set to begin at three.

It is snowing when we emerge onto the quad. The shortest route to the science building has been cordoned off, thanks to a ruptured pipeline, and the fumes are everywhere. Men in fire suits drift across the frozen grass, closing the wound in the ground, rerouting foot traffic, like astronauts patrolling virgin soil. I tuck my nose into my scarf, doing my best to economize my breaths.

Natasha opens her umbrella, lifting it high enough to shelter both of us. But the wind carries the snow under the canopy, stinging my cheeks and frosting her knees.

"I didn't realize you had an interest in birds," I say, when the stench of rotten eggs has faded.

"Oh . . . " She laughs politely, switching the umbrella stem to her other, gloveless hand. "Not really, but Professor Baum's—"

"Here." I take it from her and she thanks me, stuffing her hands into her coat pockets.

"She's a legend," Natasha continues, as I tip the canopy down against the wind. "A bunch of my friends are going."

The wind slackens, and I raise the umbrella, revealing a crowd funneling into the science building. As we move closer I pick out the president of the College, accompanied by a herd of students, Dean Barker, and Brian Russo, the custodian with whom Prue plays chess once a month.

"You guys are at 22 Grove Street, right?" Natasha says.

She must have heard about our party afterward. Given its sponsor—the Biology Department—invitations had probably gone out to senior majors.

"That's us." I hand her the umbrella, already dreading the avalanche of soiled cutlery I will have to wash tomorrow.

We merge into the throng, and Natasha drifts away from me. Most of the faces are unfamiliar, but I recognize a few colleagues, including Edson and Adaora. The lecture hall—one of the oldest at the College, its oak walls crammed with portraits of former presidents—is packed.

As I edge into the vestibule someone touches my forearm. "Ivan, is that you?"

I turn to find Morton Chowdhury, Prue's dissertation advisor—now retired—who must have driven down from Boston.

"I didn't realize you were coming," I say. "Prue will be thrilled."

They have been out of touch lately, though they had been close during her graduate years. It was through an obituary that she learned, two years ago, that his eldest daughter had died in a skiing accident. For a long time, when Prue spoke about him,

I would recognize in her face that particular dread with which my teachers addressed me after my father died. It was the same with my schoolmates. While a few of them wrote me cards, they stopped inviting me to play, as though exposure to great loss had made me radioactive.

"Wouldn't miss it," Morton says. His face is a lattice of wrinkles. They deepen as he smiles, adding, "She's the next big fish in our little pond."

He chuckles wistfully. The sound seems to designate an entire world they share, whose contours I will never know.

"I hope we manage to see it after all." I gesture at the bottleneck. "Maybe we should try the side—"

"It's him!" a small voice shrieks. I turn to find May hurtling in from the cold, her yellow backpack jouncing. As she slams against me, I almost collide with Morton.

"You promised to stop growing!" I say.

She beams up at me, showing off the serrated edge of her incoming front tooth. A beleaguered Walt—on crutches, thanks to a sprained ankle—is still picking his way toward us.

"Where's Grandpa?" she says.

"Here, somewhere. Can you spot him?"

"Walt claps my back. "Sorry, bro. Lucinda was supposed to watch her till dinner, but she bailed."

His ex-wife, he means. May, on tiptoe now, is squinting through her glasses, clouded by the sudden warmth. I unwind my scarf and wipe the lenses.

"Did you bring your notepad?" I ask her. "It might get a little boring, but you should be able to do some investigating."

Ever since Prue showed her the film version of *Harriet the Spy,* May has been fixated on joining the CIA. The ambition devastates Frank, who considers the agency a terrorist group.

"Duh I brought it!" She hops from foot to foot. "Where is he?"

"Here, somewhere. Let's find him."

We enter the hall, moving slowly to accommodate Walt. Although there are easily two hundred people in attendance, it is quieter here than in the vestibule, the chatter muted by the emerald carpet.

"How long's this supposed to go for?" Walt says, blowing his overgrown fringe out of his face.

He talks like his father—indignantly, a little sadly, without premeditation. While his parenting grates on me, I find him endearing, in part because his hopes for his life—monetary, mostly—have outlasted his failure to achieve them. He makes a reasonable living now, as the general manager of a small insurance company in Providence, though he introduces himself as a "trader." Other than one improbable return shorting penny stocks, however, his attempts to play the market have backfired.

"An hour at most, including the Q and A," I say.

I hoist May's backpack onto my shoulder, guiding her toward a row with some empty seats in the middle. The lectern, illuminated by a spotlight, stands before us like a monolith. Prue must be outside still, or late, because the two chairs beside it are empty.

"Hey," Walt shouts after us. "Look who I found!"

Frank is lurking near the fire hydrant, freshly shaven, his eyes darting from face to face. He looks so out of place here, in his old olive suit and tie, that I feel a pang of sympathy. As May drops my hand and charges toward him, dodging bodies on her way, I have the sudden impulse to sweep him out of here.

"Nice bag!" says a young man, indicating May's backpack.

"Not mine, unfortunately," I mutter, and am starting to follow her when laughter erupts from a clot of students near the podium. They are clustered around Prue, looking radiant—if overdressed—in the long blue skirt she wore to Walt's wedding. She has done her hair up in some kind of braid, which threatens to collapse as she gesticulates.

"P," I call out, after making my way down to her. She flares her eyes in greeting, and then murmurs something to one of the students, who giggles. At her throat is a pearl necklace she has never worn before.

"Did you take my phone by accident?" she says. She should be nervous, but she seems positively buzzed. As the students part, scrutinizing me, she adds, "I couldn't find it anywhere this morning."

Typical. She has a habit of losing things, or leaving them behind. To prove my innocence I hold up my phone, just as a young woman ducks in front of me, squealing, "*Hi.*"

"You made it!" Prue exclaims.

It usually charms me, how students flock to her, though now I feel a prick of envy. The contrast between our reviews on the students' underground website is a long-standing joke between us. While hers are glowing, for the most part, mine are painfully average, besting only that of Rupert Foss, professor of jurisprudence and the College's resident creep. I have always savored my low profile, taking it as proof that I have never bowed to grade inflation, or fomented a personality cult, or allowed mentorship to slacken into therapy.

Whatever the student says next is drowned out by the tinny crescendo of the activated microphone. Noboru Hayashi, the chair of Biology, has appeared behind the lectern.

"See you after," I call out, as Prue hastens toward the podium. At the same moment, Quinn sweeps her into an embrace, and I can't tell if my voice has reached her.

I slide into one of the few remaining seats and turn to scan the faces behind me, relieved to find that Walt, May, and Frank have settled a few rows back.

" . . . my privilege," Noboru is saying, "to welcome you out of the snow to a lecture my colleagues and I have long anticipated." He pauses until the only sound is Quinn rustling up the aisle.

"When I received her job application five years ago," he continues, "I knew the scientist you are about to see had extraordinary promise. I did not, however, go so far as to predict that she would design an experiment whose results have attracted global attention."

Quinn pauses at my elbow. "May I?" she mouths, pointing to the seat beside me. The smell of jasmine hangs around her.

"No problem," I whisper, standing up. She brushes past me, her bangles clinking.

The lights have dimmed. A rectangle of brightness wobbles several rows down, then disappears, as applause sweeps the room like a downpour. It persists, even after Prue has taken her post at the lectern.

"Thank you so much, Noboru, and thank you all for coming," she says. "It's an honor to be here."

She squares her papers. She is so beautiful. *My wife,* I think, as I sometimes do, as she lifts her eyes to the crowd and begins.

Five

———

Over the past few years, two very different experiments
were conducted on the same species of animal, the
vole—a cuddlier version of the mouse—and published
in leading scientific journals. The first experiment
investigated how male and female voles communicate
with one another. Using ultrasound detectors to render
their voices audible to human ears, researchers arranged
a series of ten-minute encounters between female and
male voles in small, acoustically sealed glass chambers.
The animals were surprisingly loquacious. In their
paper, published three years ago in *Behavior,* the researchers offer quantitative descriptions of the voles'
many vocalizations, charting their number, duration,
and frequency. The potential meaning of these sounds
remains unknown.

The second experiment, published in *Neuropsycho-
pharmacology*, investigated whether voles, like humans,
experience heartbreak. First the researchers played
Cupid, pairing females with males and giving them
enough time to mate and bond with one another. Five

days later, they separated the couples. Each male vole was then subjected to three situations that, under ordinary circumstances, cause voles observable distress. First, he was dropped into a beaker of tap water and forced to remain there for several minutes. Second, he was suspended by the tail in pitch darkness. Third, he was placed in a maze with no exit.

The results were striking. Compared with the control group, the voles that had been separated from their partners showed little concern for their own survival. Dangled upside down in darkness, they did not thrash like their counterparts, but simply hung there. While their counterparts paddled like mad to keep their heads above water, they floated listlessly.

What do these two experiments teach us? In one sense, the answer is straightforward. The second experiment, reminiscent of Harry Harlow's studies on maternal deprivation in monkeys, suggests that voles may serve as effective human proxies in pharmacological research on love. It is an example of what scientists call "applied," rather than "basic" research, performed in the service of understanding—and eventually treating—human brains.

The first experiment, on the other hand, represents that second dimension of science—basic research—conducted for the sole purpose of furthering knowledge about the animal in question. It demonstrates that voles, like humans, have voices, and that the apparent silence between them is actually seething with sound.

Taken together, the experiments teach us a third, less

obvious, and more important lesson. That lesson will be my subject today. It is not about voles, but about the Life Sciences, and it may have already occurred to you. How, you might be wondering, can the same field of inquiry interpret the same animal as both a communicative being and, simultaneously, a proxy for human flesh? Why, moreover, does its status as a human proxy not prevent us from torturing it?

The answer, I wager, is that the Life Sciences are pathological. Year after year, in paper after paper, we biologists interpret other animals as two contradictory phenomena: subjects of their own worlds and objects to mutilate.

This paradox has a long history. At the time of Harry Harlow's research, for example, Jane Goodall was penning her first field notes. Thirty years later, as biomedical experiments on great apes flourished, Sue Savage-Rumbaugh was launching her pioneering work into human-language learning in chimpanzees. Today, neuroscientists at Columbia are removing the eyes of baboons in order to study the etiology of strokes, even as their contemporaries publish field studies on baboon culture. What is going on here? It would be one thing if we agreed that other animals were automatons with flickering, negligible inner lives. However implausible, that position would at least make sense to an impartial observer. Yet that observer would find no such clarity in our literature. Instead, she would find a community prepared to regard the same being as both a meat machine and a creature with a voice.

Ornithologists may consider themselves immune to this critique. Even though many of us engage in biomedical research, we tend to think of ourselves as falling into the Goodall rather than the Harlow camp. We are fustier, nerdier, and considerably less rich than our colleagues in neurobiology. Yet much of our basic research, while it may not harm our subjects, still evinces a pathology of its own: narcissism. To read our studies is to confront—repeatedly—the stubborn and scientifically fatal confusion that birds are lesser versions of ourselves.

To see this fallacy in action, consider the study that helped earn me an assistant professorship at this very institution. In that experiment, my colleagues and I set out to study spatial intelligence in crows. To do this, we designed an experimental drama so familiar it has become cliché: an animal faces an obstacle to an objective and must overcome that obstacle in order to qualify as intelligent. In this case, our crows had to make a detour around a glass panel in order to reach a mound of peanuts on the other side. They passed the test with flying colors, and so did we. A reputable journal published our results, which earned us yet another grant.

But what exactly did our study achieve? Did it reveal new information about how crows think? Or did it demonstrate their ability to mimic a specifically human form of reasoning? For years, I assumed the former was true. Lately, though, I have come to suspect that what we discovered in our laboratory, with the help of our props, was fairly banal: strong evidence in favor of the crows' capacity for instrumental reason, the least sophisticated line of thinking known to man. While we had set out to investigate another animal's point of view, we instead planted a question in its mind. That question, not unfamiliar in late capitalism, was: How do I consume, faster?

Each year, practitioners of basic behavioral research spend hundreds of thousands of dollars sowing that question in the minds of millions of birds, apes, mice, and other laboratory animals. Throughout the United States and elsewhere, these beings endure Kafkaesque experimental dramas like the one our crows put up with, all in the name of intellectual inquiry. It is as though, in order to learn about other animals, we feel compelled to remake them in our image. That image is not very attractive, it turns out. The typical laboratory animal is a diminished creature, prone to the same compulsive behaviors that zoo animals often exhibit. It walks in circles, plucks out its hair, and sometimes ingests its own vomit—behaviors that almost never occur in the wild. The question should trouble us, I think: Why does the controlled study of animals so often double, by virtue of its rigor, as the practice of driving them mad?

Field research, which favors detached observation to experimental intervention, spares its subjects from this hell. And yet, like our study on crows, it demonstrates its own selection bias. The data we look for—the data that resonates with the public—tends to share the following upshot: *Look! They do what we do.* Like us, other animals have been observed to make tools; to mourn their dead; to recognize themselves in mirrors; to paint; to apply geometrical and arithmetical rules; to deceive; to commit to one partner; and even to commit suicide. Headlines like these pop up every other week. When you read them, perhaps you feel—as I once did—a frisson of delight.

Take the research suggesting that ravens have what scientists call "theory of mind"—the ability to attribute mental states to others. That data astonished me when it was published back in 2006. I sent it to all my friends. Yet something prevented me from trusting my own wonder. The feeling seemed to expose some failure in me: a lack, that is, of the very imaginative capacity—to wit, theory of mind—I was so shocked to discover in the bird.

I claim, Darwinian that I am, to know I am an animal, another twig on the tree of life. But if I *knew* this, really accepted it, I wouldn't be surprised that other animals can think beyond themselves. I would be surprised, rather, that an ape who spent over two million years in the middle of the food chain somehow managed to conquer the earth.

Our triumph is unprecedented. No other animal, over the course of the 3.8 billion years since life began, has consolidated power as we have. Even if our dominion represents just one chapter in a longer ecological story, it is a victory of staggering proportions. After tens of thousands of years as an ordinary hominid, we managed to abolish our competitors, transform our habitat, and spread it across every continent. Now we not only control the earth, but we have also developed the nuclear capacity to destroy it many times over. How did we do this? One leading hypothesis is our ability to engage in a particular activity, the same one I am engaging in right now. I refer of course to language: the activity of speech.

What exactly defines this activity has divided philosophers for centuries. Whatever the answer, it distinguishes the sounds coming out of my mouth right now from laughter, or music, or sobs. The *Encyclopedia Britannica* defines language as "a system of arbitrary vocal symbols by means of which a social group cooperates." According to most linguists, two necessary conditions of that system are the features known as "displacement" and "syntax." By "displacement," linguists mean the capacity to refer to entities outside a speaker's immediate environment. This capacity is what allows me to talk, for example, about the fall of Rome, the snow outside, and the year 2050. It is also what enables me to make sense of abstractions—such as language itself—and of entities that don't exist.

"Syntax," on the other hand, refers to the rules that govern vocal symbols. This feature of language is what enables the sounds coming out of my mouth to combine

in such a way that they form a new signification—
namely, a thought—that transcends their individual
meanings. This very sentence is one such example.
Syntax explains why a given verbalization can amount to
more than the sum of its parts.

Received wisdom holds that language is unique to
human beings. In technical terms, this is another way
of saying that syntax and displacement are unique to
human language. With the exception of bee dances,
which articulate the location of distant food, no other
animal communication system has been shown to
exhibit syntax, or to refer to objects outside the being's
immediate environment. Most linguists therefore
consider their sounds—hissing, lowing, barking, and so
forth—to be spontaneous responses to stimuli, no more
significant than human laughter. This deficit helps
explain why animals cannot think. It helps explain why
they have not ascended, as we have, into the light of
reason, but remain shackled, so to speak, to the walls of
Plato's cave.

The study that brings me here today challenges that
assumption. We found that zebra finches, like humans,
can discriminate between different configurations of the
same units of sound. Our method was simple. We began
by recording a phrase of birdsong, and then divided it
into its elementary units, known coincidentally as
"notes," which we labeled A, B, C, and D. We were able
to isolate these units with the help of a spectrogram—a
map of sound waves—on which the notes showed up as

continuous traces along a sinusoidal curve. After that, we reordered the notes to build three new phrases—BCDA, DCBA, and CDAB, respectively—which we played back to the birds. Some of the birds listened to all three phrases in silence. But most chirped at the first, flew away at the second, and squawked—with great animation—at the third. That suggests that they are sensitive not only to individual notes, but also to their configuration. It therefore provides the first experimental evidence of syntax in a nonhuman vocal system.

Our data do not prove, however, that finch songs qualify as language. To cross that Rubicon, my colleagues and I would have to discover unambiguous evidence of displacement in their melodies; to show, in other words, that—like human words—their notes can refer to objects outside their physical vicinity. There are a variety of ways we might test for this, though none are very promising. One option would be to present a group of finches with the same familiar object—a caterpillar, say—and record their vocal response. If we were to find the same note or note-sequence across all of their vocalizations, we could define this phrase, provisionally, as the finch term for "caterpillar." We could then remove the caterpillars from their environment and analyze their subsequent melodies for that same phrase. If it recurred, we would have some evidence of their ability to "talk" about absent phenomena, and therefore of displacement in their vocal system.

Yet for that evidence to carry any force, we would

have to establish that the phrase of birdsong actually signified "caterpillar." This is much easier said than done. Even if every finch uttered the same phrase in response to a given caterpillar, how would we know it wasn't saying "food"? Well, we could confront it with another treat—millet, for example—and listen for that same phrase. If the phrase recurred, we would have some evidence that it signified "food." But what if the finch repeated the phrase in response to a predator, pest, or other stimulus? How, moreover, could we be sure that it meant "food" and not "this looks good," or "this looks gross," or "thank you," or "damn you," or "let me out of here, you sick bastards"?

We scientists therefore face a paradox hitherto confined to philosophy. How do you translate a word beyond reasonable doubt without speaking the language in question? Even if we establish a strong correlation between a given phrase of birdsong and a physical object or fellow animal—as Vincent Janik, Laela Sayigh, and other cetacean biologists have done in their work on dolphins' signature whistles—we would have to assume that the phrase signified a physical object in the bird's immediate vicinity. But what if it instead signified a thought? There would be no way to establish this, empirically, because—unlike caterpillars—thoughts are unobservable. We would have to learn their languages ourselves.

That may sound like a pipe dream. But one day, the notion that the animal voices around us are talking gibberish may come to seem equally far-fetched. Whatever they may be saying, our study on syntax is hardly the first indication that it may be something more than "feed me" or "mate with me."

Consider, for example, the recent analyses of dolphin vocalizations using Zipf's law, the method researchers have long used to search for extraterrestrial intelligence. The method was invented in the 1930s by George Zipf, a linguist who discovered a pattern shared by almost all human languages: in speech, the most common word— in English, "the"—occurs twice as often as the second most common word, which occurs three times as often as the third most common word, and so on. When he plotted these words logarithmically, Zipf found that the relation between them yields a line with a slope of -1. Today, researchers at the SETI Institute use Zipf's method to test incoming signals from outer space, searching for gradients of -1 in the hope of identifying intelligent aliens.

To model what an alien language might look like, astronomers have applied Zipf's method to the sounds emitted by dolphins. To do so, they mapped each dolphin's squeaks and whistles visually, using a spectrogram, and then looked for natural gaps in the resulting sound wave. These gaps enabled them to divide the dolphin's voice into units, which they then mapped logarithmically. The resulting slope was -.95, virtually identical to that of human speech.

There is a limit, of course, to what approaches like

Zipf's can teach us. Like us, the astronomers succeeded only in plotting animal voices mathematically. Were you to apply the same method to the words I am speaking now—to record and map them visually, along a sine curve—the image would reveal no hint of what I have been saying. It would expose every nuance of my voice, but it would not compel you to think my thoughts. Unlike my words, it would provide no evidence of a mind inside my body.

Nor would it enable you to prove that I, too, could talk about the past and future, or God, or other abstractions. None of these things are empirically demonstrable. Nor is language, for that matter. I may be talking about it now, but given that my vocalizations have nothing to do with what is actually happening— nothing to do, for example, with the expressions on your faces, or the hunger in my belly, or the texture of my shirt—no scientist worth her salt would be able to show, using our methods, that I am speaking at all.

I find myself in her position, with regard to my subjects—the small, quizzical faces I confront every morning, in my laboratory here on campus. I must cut a strange figure to them, scuttling around with my clipboard, blasting messages out of a small black box. Day after day, they watch my colleagues and me pore over these messages. They might find it amusing, if they experience such a thing, to know that we have no idea what they mean.

Our position is curious. Some future species may

share it one day, when they discover the ruins of our libraries. If the oceans haven't wiped the volumes clean by then, they will find traces not only of our bibles and constitutions, but also of our symphonies. Perhaps they will take an interest in these primitive dots and lines—measuring their width, height, and so on—and believe that in doing so, they have discovered music, even as they work all the while in silence.

If we succeed, one day, in translating birdsong into English, language will share the fate of that other fallen idol: tool use. It will no longer provide evidence of our superiority, but rather of our kinship with the beings that surround us. Will we find other ways to convince ourselves that we are the enlightened animals, when we are no longer the only animals that speak? What, if anything, will distinguish us?

Perhaps the finches will tell us. They may have a ready answer, though I doubt, for my part, that we will like what they have to say.

Six

The applause begins cautiously at first, then swells. She collects her papers, blushing as someone whistles.

"So that's what she's had up her sleeve," Quinn whispers.

I force my hands together a few times, my fingers numb, as the room floods with queasy yellow light. Then I stare at my knees, the twilled cotton of my chinos. She has lost it. She has lost her mind.

"We have time for a few questions," Noboru calls out. "A microphone should be circulating—Lucas, can you—? Oh, terrific. Thanks." He scans the room.

People glance at one another. I will them not to speak, or laugh. *Good God, let this be over,* I think. Then I remember the party.

"Right there, in the back." Noboru gestures.

A young woman in a toffee-colored blazer stands up, and the student hands her the mic.

"That was super-interesting," she says, "but I'm a little confused. How do you plan to decode the finches' tweets, or, sorry, their *cheeps*"—scattered laughter—"without a Rosetta stone, or something? Also, if they really do have thoughts, how do you feel about keeping them in your laboratory?"

Prue is a slight person, and in the glare of the spotlight she looks even thinner. I hold my breath.

"Would you like my job?" she says. "Because you've just posed the two questions that haunt me every day. I may have shown that the finches' vocal system has syntax, but by what stretch of the imagination have I convinced myself that I could ever find a way into its semantic register? And even if I could, what makes me think the birds would want to speak to me, their prison warden?"

There is a round of uneasy laughter. But she continues, unabashed: "That second question is the reason I only keep any group of birds for three months, at most, before releasing them back into their home regions. As for the question of how we might translate their songs, I really don't know. There are times when the attempt strikes me as a fool's errand. But the notion that a vocal system would have syntax, but no semantics, seems even more absurd to me. We've found strong evidence that these birds are saying something. I want to find out what."

"How?" someone calls out. A young voice, probably a student's. The dean turns and glares. There is a tittering.

"Shall we move on?" Noboru suggests, but Prue lifts her hand.

"It's all right. I was just going to add that, with the help of our heroic librarian"—she gestures toward someone in the first row, who nods deeply—"Amina Singh, we have published an expanding online archive of their melodies. The data is public, available to any linguists, cryptographers, musicians, and other researchers interested in analyzing them."

She smiles brightly, as though she has not just accused her colleagues of torture. As Noboru calls on someone else, a familiar, unkind thought strikes me: *As smart as Prue is, as graceful as she is, there is something ridiculous about her.*

"You mentioned Sue Savage-Rumbaugh's research on language learning in apes," the next questioner says. Twisting around, I find it is Clarice Hussein, a colleague of mine who works on Hume. "I'm curious: Why not go that route? Instead of treating birdsong as a text to decode, why not create an artificial lingua franca and try to communicate with your finches that way?"

As she sits back down I catch sight of Walt a few seats away from her, texting. May, pen in hand, shoots me a furtive wave.

"It's a great question," Prue says. "And I do admire that work. It's profound for a number of reasons, especially in demonstrating that the qualities that seem to make us most human—the capacity for symbolic communication, for instance—are not uniquely human at all. But it doesn't address nonhuman vocal systems on their own terms. That's what I'm after. If we could translate these vocal systems, we could test the Sapir-Whorf hypothesis anew, with respect to animal languages. Does one's language dictate one's reality, as Sapir and Whorf claimed it does for human tongues? What would the world look like, through the lens of birdsong?"

A man rises and edges toward the aisle, forcing half a row of people to stand. Heads turn. It is Jeremiah Wood, also a biologist, who championed Prue's application to the College five years ago. Prue does not waver, though I see her see him clear the gallery and exit through the double doors.

"The political ramifications would be Copernican," she says. "And very uncomfortable, I would guess. Like the doctrine of manifest destiny, our dominance might begin to strike us as a vast, coordinated crime, rather than a logical expression of our superiority."

I begin to feel the pressure of other eyes. An administrator near the door glances gingerly in my direction. Another colleague, three rows ahead, meets my gaze before feigning interest in the wall clock. *Her husband,* I imagine him thinking. *How must it feel to watch her bite the hand that feeds her?*

The next question comes from John Sawyer, professor emeritus of linguistics: "Yes, good afternoon and congratulations on your findings. May I suggest, with all due respect, that you are jumping the gun here? Syntax and displacement are only two of the many features a vocal system would have to exhibit in order to qualify as language. I have read your study. Your team showed that finches have a limited ability to construct phrases and identify differences in sound order, presumably in order to attract mates, repel rivals, and establish territory. You offer no evidence that birds can generate new sounds or new configurations of sounds, let alone in a recursive fashion. As for the research Clarice mentioned, let us not forget its fall from grace after a brief heyday in the seventies. The vast majority of ape language experiments were intellectually bankrupt, archetypes of the Clever Hans effect."

No tittering, this time. Only a shifting, the murmur of bodies. Noboru manages a look of vague bewilderment.

"Has anyone heard of Clever Hans?" Prue says. A student in the front row nods maniacally. God knows what she is after now.

"He was a horse who gained fame in the early 1900s for apparently solving arithmetical problems by stamping his foot. It turned out that what he was actually doing, unbeknownst to his trainer, was watching his human audience so closely that he inferred from their body language when to stop stamping. That the scientific community concluded that he was a fraud, rather than an emotional savant, is a perfect example of the kind of hubris I tried to bring out in my lecture."

"Are you defecting from science, then?" Sawyer calls out, sparking another bout of rustling. "Forgive me, but I don't understand."

"I love science." Prue draws a breath, finally ruffled. "That's why I think it's worthy of critique. Mapping birdsong mathematically will never prove that birds have language. As accurate as our spectrograms may be, they provide no information about whether the finches' melodies meet the standards you mentioned, John." She smiles to herself. "My husband works on this, actually—it's a problem in epistemology: the gap between our data and the truth."

Quinn nudges me, and I shrink down in my seat. *Please, my love. Don't drag me into this.*

"That old fable, about a group of blind men touching different parts of an elephant?" she presses on. "The ones touching the tusks arguing that it's hard and smooth, the ones touching the end of the tail saying it's coarse, and so on. . . . Well, I think our species represents one of those blind men, confined by our language to one region of the elephant, one view of things. We have a philosophical imperative to change that."

A wet, ropy cough issues from behind me. Without looking, I can tell that it has come from Frank. Here is his chance to interpose himself, deflect attention from her, something I never thought I'd wish for.

But he doesn't, and now Noboru intervenes: "We have time

for one last question. . . ." A hand shoots up ahead of me, and he brightens. "In the middle, yes."

A shuffling, as the microphone is passed.

"I think it's magnificent," the questioner booms. "Your implication—that we're not the wiser animals, but the demented ones. That insanity, not wisdom, explains our dominance."

Dalton. His legs are crossed, one arm draped across the back of the neighboring seat, probably occupied by someone he doesn't even know.

"Not *Homo sapiens,* but *Homo infirmum,*" he adds. "Why else would we have vandalized the earth?"

Give me a fucking break, I think. As I close my eyes Quinn whispers, "He's great."

"You've raised the question of what other animals might say to us, if we would listen," he continues. "What, I wonder, would you say to them?"

"Ah . . ." Prue smiles mischievously. "Good question. I don't know. Forgive me?"

The reference to his book title prompts a ripple of warm laughter from the in-the-know.

"Fair enough," he says. I could break his knees.

Noboru announces the conclusion of the lecture, triggering a final spasm of applause. I am out of my seat before it is finished, jostling past Quinn and up the aisle. May and Walt are putting on their coats, but Frank is still gazing ahead, beatific, hands steepled under his chin.

"Let's get out of here before the rush," I hear myself say, handing May her backpack. To Frank I add: "Where did Prue park?"

He ignores me. The woman beside him, trapped by his knees, taps his shoulder.

"Uncle Ivan, guess what!" May brandishes her notepad. "I made—"

"Do you?" I interrupt, turning to Walt.

Walt shrugs. "Shouldn't we . . . ?" He gestures toward the podium.

"I'll meet you outside," I say, giving up on them. Dodging bodies, I charge through the side exit and out, into the whiteness.

Part II

Seven

———

Dear Prue,

Pardon my absence at tonight's gathering. I had been looking
forward to celebrating you. Noboru spoke for the Department in
praising your team's experiment, and we all know what a pivotal role
you played in designing it. Your discussion of the results would have
been the capstone of a distinguished tenure file.

It is therefore with a good deal of confusion and regret that I confess
I no longer plan to support your tenure case. Your remarks today
made that impossible.

You implied, in a public forum, that our work is tantamount to animal
abuse. The accusation is not just unfounded. It is dangerous. It
bolsters the case of the many interests who would like to see our
discipline go down the drain. Coming from anyone, it would have been
dismaying. From the mouth of a scientist I have described to others as
the future doyenne of ornithology, it was a shock.

Forgive me for being blunt. I had no idea you felt this way. I am shaken—and, quite frankly, hurt—that you chose to take us down with you.

Sincerely,
Jeremiah

The email is time-stamped 4:57, just under an hour ago. It is the first thing I see when I open Prue's laptop in the kitchen, the party already under way, to download a computer game for May.

She must have opened it, because an empty draft is saved below the text, its cursor pulsing. Painful to read, no doubt, though Jeremiah put it more gently than I would have. After today, she may as well kiss tenure goodbye.

Her laughter wafts in from the living room, above the ebb and swell of talk, sounding forced. We have hardly spoken since the lecture. After locating our car I pulled around to the front of the building, waiting in the warmth while she said her goodbyes. A group of students intercepted her first, followed by the College president. As she thanked them Frank trailed her, seeming not to notice the people clustered near the entrance to the hall, whispering. Their faces asked the same questions that were engulfing me, namely: Who does she think she is? And: How much longer will it take for the pageantry to fade, for the damage to come to light? They were questions she seemed to have absorbed, at least subliminally, when she spotted the car and met my eye, her smile laced with fatigue. I stepped out and managed a brief, congratulatory hug before shepherding Frank, May, and Walt into the backseat.

"A lady picked her nose!" May announced. She licked the remains of the snowball Walt packed for her outside, adding: "She picked her nose and wiped it under the seat and I saw it. I have proof. I did a whole report, like in the CIA."

I glanced in the rearview mirror, expecting Frank to groan at the mention of the agency. But he was staring out the window, his eyes bright.

"Read it to us, sweetie," Prue said, as we circled the quad. "Tell us what you found out."

"Okay, um . . ." May studied her notebook. "Oh yeah, here. The guy with the wrinkly neck whispered something to the lady next to him. I didn't hear what he said, though. The lady scratched her eyebrow with her pinky. She has weird hair. Then—oh, then, the guy next to me bit off his thumbnail and blew it off his tongue. *Gross.*" She looked up. "That was almost as disgusting as the booger!"

"Don't forget your present for Grandpa, bug," Walt murmured.

"Oh yeah!" From her backpack May produced a rose of crinkled tissue, affixed to a green pipe cleaner. Frank, finally distracted from his musings, crowed his admiration, then tucked it into his breast pocket.

"Wait, Aunt Prue?" May said.

"Yes, honey?"

Prue, seated in the passenger seat beside me, was picking furiously at her cuticles. From the way she kept glancing at me, I could tell she was hoping I would offer some reaction to the speech, positive or otherwise, and felt a flicker of satisfaction at my refusal to indulge her.

"What do you call the thing you were standing behind?" May said, through a mouthful of snow.

"A lectern."

"Okay. Aunt Prue takes her notes off the lectern. Everybody cheers. Everybody loves Aunt Prue. The end!"

By now two dozen guests have arrived—Biology faculty, mostly, along with a handful of students—congregating in the hall and living room. Dalton, mercifully, is not among them. Morton left after only a few minutes, citing the weather, followed by Edson and Adaora. Though he rarely accepts our invitations, the pianist from upstairs—Josip Milak—has arrived, keeping mostly to himself.

After downloading May's game I pop an antacid, waiting for her to emerge from the bathroom. Her voice wafts through the locked door, humming the theme song to Snoopy: a recent obsession she must have picked up at school. The melody calms me. All I want is to get Prue alone, which won't be possible for at least another hour. The guests have barely made a dent in the hors d'oeuvres. A tray of chicken samosas is still on the counter, its cellophane slick with lamplight. The pigs in blankets we put out earlier have gone mostly untouched, though they tend to disappear. Maybe these will fare better.

I am peeling the cellophane off the platter when two voices separate from the throng—Quinn's, and a male voice I don't recognize. They have reached the corridor now, approaching the kitchen.

". . . didn't know she had a cri de coeur in store for us," says the man.

"I loved it, but her husband practically had a conniption," Quinn says, discreetly. "He was sitting right beside me."

"Who's she married to, again?"

"Ivan Link? He teaches here."

"Oh, I don't . . ."

"Epistemologist. I'm sure you've—"

"Wait, *that* guy?"

My heart leaps into my throat.

"You're kidding," the man is saying.

"Don't be rude. And keep your voice down. This is his house."

"Maybe we can find all the poles he keeps up his ass."

They enter the kitchen, where I have knelt before a cupboard with my back to the door, rummaging noisily.

"Ivan!" Quinn exclaims.

"Nice to see you," I stand up, pot in hand. My ears burn.

"Great party." She smiles with horror. "Can I help?"

The man beside her is bald, with pasty skin and a sheepish look. He takes a generous sip of wine, avoiding my gaze.

"Da duh-duh-duh-*da!*" May sings, bursting through the bathroom door. As Quinn and the man chuckle at her she shrinks behind me, pushing her glasses up her nose.

"Did you need something?" I say to Quinn, as the man slips into the bathroom.

"No, we were just . . ." She gestures after him, glancing at the pot in my hand. May gambols toward the laptop, humming again as she loses herself to the game.

"I'll see you out there, then," I say, and set the pot on the stove. When I turn back, Quinn is hastening into the corridor.

Still smarting, I wait a moment, and then carry the tray of samosas into the living room. The guests have clustered near the darkened French windows or draped themselves over the couches. Walt has his arm slung around Jeffrey Sato, a visiting plant biologist on leave from Tokyo University. Josip is paging through a book of photographs we keep, in lieu of a television, on our vintage balsa console.

A man I don't recognize tosses an olive pit onto the coals in the fireplace, muttering something that prompts a whinnying laugh from the woman beside him. The fire I built when we got home has shrunken to a few liquid orange threads.

Setting the platter down on the free end of the beverage table, I notice Prue leaning against the bookcase. Her elaborate hairdo is sagging now, haloed by frizz. A young man in tight black jeans is talking to her—or *at* her, rather—flapping his hands as he speaks.

"Everything you said, it's just . . ." He gestures around the room. "We're a cancer, a cancer on the earth. There are lots of initiatives going on, I don't know if you've heard. Green Campus is hosting a sit-in next week, as part of the divestment campaign. If you want to get involved, I can put you in touch with Kyle. . . ."

Prue glances at her phone and then past him, catching my eye. *Rescue me,* her expression says. I shoot her a look that says, *You dug your grave, now lie in it.* Satisfied, I head back to the kitchen, only to find myself face to face with the bald man. With a stiff nod he sidesteps me, wiping his palms on his jeans.

The front doorbell rings. When I open the door, Natasha is standing there, shivering, her eyelashes crusted with snow. She must have walked here, because her scarf is soaked.

"Come in, please." I help her out of her coat. "Can I get you a drink?"

"Wine would be great." She tucks a curl behind her ear. "Whatever you have."

I return to the kitchen to stow her coat in the mudroom, only to discover Frank hunched over the counter, glaring down at a Home Depot catalog. May, still glued to Prue's laptop, is singing to herself.

"Everything all right?" I say, pouring myself a second glass of wine.

Instead of answering, Frank flips a page of the catalog so abruptly that it tears. His hands are trembling. May's flower droops from his pocket.

"Why don't I introduce you to some of our colleagues?" I say, regretting the offer as soon as it leaves my lips.

He scowls. "They didn't get it."

"Didn't get—"

"The *speech*." He stares at me. With a flourish of his hand he adds, "Schmoozing out there, like nothing happened. Like she never said a goddamn word."

I glance at May, then back at him, but he only sniffs. I say, quietly, "I think it went over surprisingly well."

He shoves the catalog across the counter, so violently that it slides off the far edge. Then he licks both forefingers, smoothing them over his tufted eyebrows. There is a fresh ink stain on his suit, bleeding from one of the many pens he keeps in his breast pocket.

Before I can point it out he barrels past me and back into the party. I retrieve the catalog and follow him, worried he is about to make a scene, but he veers into his room.

". . . from the Himalayas, I think," Natasha is saying, when I return with her merlot. Noboru, a consummate flirt, has cornered her near the piano.

She accepts the glass and adds, for my benefit, "I was just telling him about this myth we read, in my anthropology class, about the origin of language?" She swills her wine, smiling. "You've probably heard it."

"Try me," I say, charmed—to my surprise—by her simpering tone. Then again, it is probably the alcohol.

"The first human beings had two mouths," she says, "just like they had two eyes, nostrils, and ears. The first mouth chewed and spat and sucked, while the other breathed. One day the skin between them tore, leaving a cleft here"—she taps the furrow between her nose and upper lip.

Her lip gloss is coral red, applied so liberally it has clumped near the corners of her mouth. As she gesticulates, basking in our attention, I feel a twinge of sympathy. While she has mentioned various friends of hers during our meetings, I have only ever seen her walking alone across campus, weighted down by her viola. This party will probably be the highlight of her weekend.

". . . the two mouths had to contend with each other," she is saying now. "One representing desire, the other harmony. Speech is the thunder of their collision, they say. The quarrel of appetite and law."

"Sounds like Freud had a plagiarist," Noboru says. With his free hand, he reaches for a samosa, tilting his paper plate. A lone blueberry rolls across it, curbed by a smear of hummus.

"Was one, more likely," I say.

Natasha hesitates, glancing at me.

"You ever been analyzed?" Noboru asks her, through a mouthful of samosa.

Without warning, her hand darts to my left shoulder, swiping something off my back. When I stiffen, she retracts it, adding: "Just some chalk, from class before."

I peer over my shoulder, only to find a ghostly smear down the whole of my blazer. Noboru whistles.

"Hang on, let me take care of this," I say, and set down my wine. Why hadn't Prue said something?

"Oh, professor?" Natasha calls after me. When I turn she says, "I have a draft of my next chapter—I was wondering if I could send it to you?"

I nod—too curtly, I realize, because she practically cringes as she adds, "Any chance you'll be in your office this weekend, so we can go over my first one?"

As a TA, Natasha has been granted a key to the Philosophy building, though she is supposed to limit herself to normal work hours. She says, "I was planning to work there on Sunday."

"I won't be, unfortunately," I say, choosing to overlook her tacit confession. "But let's definitely meet next week."

She thanks me, and I head for the bedroom, pausing on the

way to feed the catalog into the fire. The flames roar back to life, eating through an image of a lawn mower. With the poker I wedge it under the grate, calmed by the sudden heat. My indigestion is fading, at long last. In its place is a sharpening hunger.

"Hey, bro?" Walt calls out.

He is hovering over the beverage table, balancing on one crutch as he tops off his martini. The table, crowded with open bottles, is positioned dangerously close to the piano.

"You good with May?" He smacks his nicotine gum. A flake of pastry clings to his goatee.

"I just called a car," he adds, screwing the cap on the bottle of Absolut. "Dinner date with Julia in twenty."

"When can we meet her?" I drag the table a few inches toward the wall, making the bottles clink.

"If I don't fuck it up, you mean," he says.

As he gulps down the vodka May gallops into view, falling to her stockinged knees just in time to slide across the floor, up to his feet. A few guests applaud. Embarrassed, she wraps her arms around Walt's shin.

"The computer froze," she whines. "I was in the middle of a level."

With a flick of her head, she propels her dark bangs—badly in need of a trim—out of her eyes. To me, she adds: "Aunt Prue's on the phone. She said to get you."

"Let's go fix it," I say, as Walt's phone dings. He plucks the olive from his martini and, to my horror, offers it to May, who pops it in her mouth.

"That's my ride." He sets his glass on the piano. "See you tomorrow, bug. Be good."

May takes my hand. Together we turn back toward the kitchen, pausing to pour her the cup of ginger ale Prue supposedly promised her. As she gulps it down I pave a paper plate with four layers of prosciutto, a trapezoid of Brie, and two pigs in blankets for myself. If Prue can send herself up in flames, why shouldn't I?

"If we're lucky, it'll remember where you were," I say, when we have returned to the kitchen. I restart the laptop, stuffing the last of the ham into my mouth.

"Why are you eating so fast?" May says.

"Sorry." I cover my mouth. "Want some?"

She scrunches up her face.

"How about dessert?"

But she is staring past me, into the living room. Not until I follow her gaze do I notice that the rest of the house has gone silent.

Eight

When we emerge from the kitchen the guests are standing where they were, motionless as a tableau vivant. Most of them still have drinks in hand, though no one is speaking. They are all facing the french windows.

Frank is blocking them, his head near the ceiling. He must be standing on something, but the couch is blocking my view of his feet. His hands are raised before him, trembling. They are holding something. Something moving.

It is Rex, struggling to free himself. His wings are crushed against his body, his head twitching. One pinkish leg stamps in midair.

"Let me put it this way," Frank says. "Why, exactly, should I *not?*"

I look from face to face, and see a mix of confusion and alarm. Rex, meanwhile, has opened his beak. He might be shrieking, if Frank's thumb weren't pressed against his throat.

"Come on," Frank says. "You're a civilized bunch. Who can give me a good reason?"

A croaking sound, barely audible, issues from Rex. Frank adjusts his grip. His cheeks are flushed, but he has not raised his voice.

"The clock is ticking, folks," he says. "And don't bother citing some right to life, unless you omnivores are prepared to explain why you have no qualms about eating chickens."

May shrinks against me. I whisper, "You stay here."

She nods. I edge along the wall, the better to startle him from the side.

"It doesn't belong to you," someone calls out: Natasha, ever the eager student. I scan the room for Prue, and instead lock eyes with Quinn, who raises her eyebrows. Noboru approaches her, murmuring something.

"Doesn't *belong* to me," Frank repeats. "Is that the best you can do? Anyone else want to weigh in here? You're all scholars, aren't you? Give me one good reason why I shouldn't kill this goddamn beast."

A loud groan sounds, suddenly, followed by a series of cracks. Frank glances downward. He is standing on our console, which he has dragged over from the couch—hardly strong enough to support our art books, let alone a man. He seems to realize this, and hesitates.

"Let me help you down, Frank," I say, beside him now.

His Adam's apple glints with sweat. Instead of answering he disengages his right hand and, still gripping Rex, draws a fountain pen from his breast pocket. Rex takes the opportunity to wriggle one wing free. It flaps, uselessly.

"What do I have here?" Frank says. With his teeth, he yanks off the cap, flinging it my way. I dodge. He brandishes the pen, the tapered metal point catching the lamplight.

He says, "What are you all, lobotomized?"

Rex is croaking again. His wing catches the tissue of May's flower, nudging it free. It lands headfirst on the hardwood.

"What you are looking at"—Frank stabs the air—"is the deadliest weapon of all time. It's what we've used to terrorize our fellow creatures, tyrannize our fellow man, and spread our smoke and steel across this naked earth."

May whimpers. She has crawled under the piano, though her eyes are fixed on Frank. I have to get her out of here.

"Fireworks," he continues, as I jog toward her, "fire extinguishers, linoleum, perfume, upholstery, brake fluid, car tires, asphalt, car seats, fabric softener, wallpaper, crayons, candles, rugs, shampoo, lipstick, candy, photographic film, footballs, fertilizer, paintbrushes, paint, toothpaste, toothbrushes, plastic bags, piano keys, my shoes . . ."

He draws a long, shuddering breath, then barks: "What do all those things have in common?"

I crouch down in front of the piano, blocking May's view of him. Terrified, she scrambles into my arms.

"Cows," Frank shouts. "Cow parts. Sometimes horses, too. Boiled bones and hearts and skin."

Rex has stopped struggling. As I carry May across the room I see him peer over Frank's thumb, his chest heaving.

"Our world is their afterlife," Frank continues. "Does no one see it? Subtract them, and we'd have nothing."

Prue appears in the mouth of the corridor.

"What's going on?" She glances at May, who buries her face in my shoulder.

"Your dad . . ." I begin, but she is already taking in the scene.

"Fuck," she whispers.

"We've forgotten that the same thing that's looking out of here"—Frank aims the pen at his temple—"is looking out of here." In one swift motion, he points the tip at Rex's eye.

As Prue pushes past us, he adds: "We're hypocrites, just like my daughter said. Not just the scientists, but all of us. Bandaging rabbits at the animal clinic and sautéing them at the brasserie."

"*Dad*," Prue says.

"That's God's image for you." He raises his voice. "That's us."

Something in the air unclenches. The guests begin to shift. As Prue strides forward they clear a path between her and Frank, who has lifted his chin in an effort not to see her.

"Get down," she snaps.

"If God's image built the abattoir," he is saying, "then God's not someone I want to meet."

I deposit May in the study. "You sit tight, okay?" I say. "I'll be right back."

She nods, stricken, as I close the door and tear back down the corridor.

A ring has formed around Prue and Frank, who is sweating harder. The pen, still aimed at Rex, shudders in his hand.

"Pain is pain is pain," he is shouting. "It isn't any kinder, when it isn't in your body."

"Dad, listen to me," Prue says, right in front of him now. "On the count of three, you're going to hand me the—"

"You said it yourself," he adds, finally hoarse. There are tears in his eyes. "What we're doing isn't right."

As I come up behind her she grabs his elbow, and he staggers back, nearly dropping the pen.

"Wait," he hisses. Then he kicks her in the ribs.

The room gasps. She stumbles against me, holding her side. I wrap my arms around her, but she shrugs me off, cursing.

"Who cares if they can talk, when they can suffer?" Frank cries out.

Headlights sweep across the glass, backlighting him. How absurd we must appear from outside, captive to a man we outnumber.

"It's time to face what we're doing, folks." Frank swallows fiercely. "What civilization's all about."

In his face is a painful clarity. He draws back the pen, aiming the tip at Rex's throat.

"Wait!" I shout. Without thinking I lift my knee, bringing my heel down hard on the console.

The wood buckles. With a look of pure surprise, Frank pitches forward into my arms. I stagger back under his weight, but manage to cushion his fall. Rex has broken free, meanwhile, squawking as the guests take cover.

Nine

———

"Can you stand up?" I say.

Frank is slumped against me on the floor, bending and unbending his knee. He nods. Across his jaw is a ripening scratch.

"I'll take that." I indicate the pen. He hands it over, allowing me to help him up and shepherd him toward the corridor.

A familiar scent is coming from him—not sweet, but not stale, either—the first time I remember him smelling this way. *Like my mother,* I think suddenly. *Like the dying.* As we cross the room the guests' eyes swarm us, pitying now, and shameless as flies to a corpse.

"Show's over," Prue calls out, with an empty laugh.

People drift toward her, murmuring. Others gather their coats. Three students, Natasha among them, linger behind the piano, making no effort to hide their fascination. Rex has settled on the mantel, preening furiously.

When we reach the guest room I turn on the Tiffany lamp. Frank lowers himself onto the unmade bed.

LINDSAY STERN

"They don't care," he says. The words come out thick, as though welling up from deep inside him.

"You . . ." I begin, but no predicate comes to mind. His duffel bag lies open on the rug, belching undershirts.

"They suffer." Frank looks up at me, surprised. "They're suffering, and no one cares."

His shirt bellies out over his pants, its lower button undone, exposing the pale, fallen ripples of his stomach.

"What were you thinking?" I whisper. A stupid question. He hadn't been thinking: that was the point.

"At least we have the concept 'pain,'" he says. "We can float above it that way, give it a purpose. But when they suffer, there is nothing but suffering. Pain is all there is."

"What's the matter with you?"

He swallows. As I turn away he points a quivering finger at my hand. A pearl of ink has skated from the tip of the pen onto my palm, branching across the skin between my thumb and forefinger.

"God damn it." I yank three tissues from the box on the dresser. Wrapping them around the tip, I add, "I hope you're satisfied, Frank. I don't think the eggheads will want anything more to do with your daughter after today."

He searches my face, looking frightened. Before he can say anything else I retreat into the hallway, closing the door firmly behind me.

Natasha has left, along with most of the other guests. Only a few people linger around Prue, helping her stack dirty glasses. Quinn crouches before the ruined console, mopping up the splinters with a dampened paper towel.

"*Satujin misui datta. Un, kakutē rupā tī de. Iya, tori o,*" says Jeffrey Sato, speaking into his phone as he pulls on his overcoat. "*Satsujin misui to ittemo* satsutori *o itta hō ga ii kamo.*"

With a curt nod in my direction, he hastens past me and through the front door. Snow blows in from the darkness.

I shiver, about to duck into the closet for a garbage bag when I notice May's trampled flower. It has been kicked to the edge of the fireplace, where a few lone embers are swimming through the ash. I kneel down and rescue it, peeling back the stiff white petals.

"Where is she?" says Prue. She steps around me to tip a plate of half-eaten canapés into the trash, her skirt grazing my shoulder.

"May? In the study. How is it?" I nod toward her rib but she only shrugs, pursing her lips. *You rest, I'll handle this*, I almost say, but I am afraid if I do she will cry.

Josip has taken a seat at the piano. He leafs through our stack of sheet music, a relic of the lessons I bought Prue on our second anniversary. She seemed grateful at the time, though I sensed it turned her hobby into a chore. We haven't tuned the thing in years.

Noticing me watching him, Josip offers a shy wave.

"Please," I say. "Treat us." But he has already begun.

"HE WAS GOING TO HURT HIM," May sobs from the study, where Prue is tucking her in on the pullout couch. "He was going to hurt Rex."

Prue murmurs something I can't hear.

The apartment is ours again, finally, though Josip has only just left. While he played I picked my way across the frozen snow to lodge the broken console in the dumpster. The remaining detritus was manageable: stained plates, rogue cutlery, an orphaned scarf. Rex regarded me stonily as I moved about, dropping anything disposable into a garbage bag.

He is still pacing the top of the bookcase, warbling to himself, despite my efforts to goad him down with a mop. The room is tidy now, but still awash in remembered noise. May's watercolors, my graduate diploma, and the framed wedding photo of Nadia and Frank—looking almost handsome, with his rakish grin— carry none of their usual warmth.

"Aunt Prue?" May says woozily, as I pass the study on the way to our bedroom.

"What is it?"

"Where do we go, when we go to sleep?"

"Nowhere, sweetheart. You stay right here."

Thirsty for air, I crack open the bedroom window. The snow has relented, but it has gotten colder. A half-moon casts a bluish light over the telephone wires, the chimneys and, in the distance, the spire of the College chapel. Our street is carpeted in white, broken by two shallow troughs. A pair of red lights glow at the southern end, then disappear.

"It's freezing in here," Prue says.

As I turn she brushes past me, toward the bureau. She has let down her hair. Bits of mascara speckle the skin under her eyes.

I close the window. "How's your rib?"

"Fine. Bruised, I think." She draws a breath, letting me kiss her. Then she unbuttons her blouse, prodding a spot on her left side. I crouch down to inspect it, but find no discoloration.

"Is your dad asleep?"

"I don't know. I don't want to think about him right now, honestly." She unclasps her necklace and then her bra, flinging it into the hamper. As she unzips her skirt she continues, despite herself: "He keeps insisting he's taking his meds, but there's no way. He must be having some kind of breakdown."

I sit down on the bed and pull off my dress shoes. She laughs bitterly, then says: "I knew something like this would happen. I should never have let him come."

"Don't blame yourself."

"I'm going to call his psychiatrist in the morning. Maybe we can get him on lithium."

Her skirt falls to the floor, its fabric pooling on the rug. Her body looks fuller than usual, more radiant, and despite or because of today's catastrophe I have the sudden urge to take her in my arms.

"I've never heard him go off on this animal rights stuff before." She pulls off her underwear, steadying herself against the wall. "He's always said he was a vegetarian for health reasons. I mean, did you see that coming?"

There are a lot of things about today I didn't see coming, I almost say. Instead I blow out my cheeks.

"Can I ask you something?" she says, as I move toward the closet. Without waiting for a reply she adds: "How did he get up there, to begin with?"

"Up where?" I fold my clothes and step into a fresh T-shirt and sweatpants. Out of habit, I think of my monograph, momentarily forgetting that I submitted it early this morning. The fact should liberate me, but instead it fills me with vertigo. My last shot at a major house, no less. Why hadn't I proofread it one more time?

"You know," Prue is saying, when I turn back toward her. "Dragging the cabinet over and speechifying, like that. Weren't you there? Didn't you see him?"

Her tacit indictment—*You let him hurt me*—hits me like a bad smell. I sputter, almost laughing: "I was in the kitchen with May."

She pelts her tights toward the hamper and misses.

"I'm the one who put a stop to it, finally," I add.

"Okay." Without bothering to retrieve them, she moves into the bathroom, running her toothbrush under the tap.

"Christ, Prue." I pick up the tights myself.

"I said, *okay*."

"Where were *you*?"

"In here, actually," she says, through a mouthful of tooth-paste. "I was on the phone with Daora."

I slide into bed, still wounded. "She was here earlier. Couldn't you have done your talking then?"

"For a second." She spits into the basin. "I don't think she would have come at all if it hadn't been for Edson."

Of the two of them, Adaora is the more mercurial, with a mordant wit that balances Edson's politesse. She was Prue's first friend here. With the exception of a falling-out last year—about which Prue had been vague—they have never fought before.

"Look, I don't mean to take this out on you." She sighs. "I'm just confused. She's really pissed about my speech."

"Why on earth would anyone be pissed about your speech?" I say, but she doesn't catch my sarcasm. She frowns, cracking her knuckles, a habit she knows I can't stand.

"I mean, I get it," she says. "Edson's a neuroscientist, and I didn't exactly sing their praises. But for god's sake, I wasn't talking about him specifically." She disappears into her closet, and then emerges, pulling her silk nightdress over her head.

Like water, the silk tumbles over her breasts. Its yellow has dimmed over the years, enough to disclose two darknesses, hardening now at the touch of the fabric. Again, I have to fight the urge to pull her down and let our bodies say all that has to be said.

"But it was my moment," she is saying. "And it's not like I put him out of a job. I gave a lecture at a liberal arts college. Everyone will have forgotten about it by next week. I mean, do you think he has a right to be angry?"

"I don't think he's the only one who has a right to be angry," I say, surprised at how casual I sound, given my thumping heart. "You put yourself out of a job today, you know."

She recoils. "Excuse me?"

"Your tenure case. You destroyed it."

She stares at me, evenly. Her eyes are hard, but something vivid, close to triumph, flashes through them.

"I don't know what you're talking about," she says. "The speech isn't even part of my file, and—"

"Yes, it was *your* moment," I interrupt. "All the more reason to discuss your work, rather than indict your discipline."

"Is this a joke?" She frowns. "Are you actually yelling at me right now?"

"I'm not yelling."

She picks up her skirt. "I did discuss my work, as a matter of fact, which you'd know if you'd have—"

"Sure." I toss my hand. "Your work. Or should I say, a 'fallacy in action,' as you put it. *And* Plato, and the Pleistocene, and fucking grieving rats. And all in the name of loving science!" I can't help but laugh, remembering her response to John Sawyer during the Q and A.

"*Voles*. Get it right." She whips me with the skirt, her eyes glittering. This could be foreplay, after all. When has our bickering not resolved in sex? Well, she has missed that boat.

"As for your diatribe against applied research," I say, scooting up against the headboard, "I don't even know where to begin. Your own father's health depends on the work of the neuroscientists you scolded."

"Actually, there's very little evidence that animal models—"

"For Christ's sake, Prue." She has been talking all day, and now it is my turn. "What the hell was your endgame? Revolutionary science?"

She blinks. "I was trying to say something new."

"Really? I never would have guessed."

My voice is shrill. This is the closest I have come in recent memory to shouting at her, but she seems less angry than exhilarated.

She says, "I didn't want to regurgitate—"

"If you want to say something new," I break in, "don't do it by calling your colleagues torturers. There are a lot of people who want to see your discipline go down the drain. How could you—"

"So you're *spying* on me now?"

With a chill of embarrassment I realize I have echoed Jeremiah's note. Before she can mount an offensive, I say: "You were afraid your dad would interrupt your lecture? I wish he had, to be honest. I was mortified, sitting there. You sounded so goddamn spoiled. The Biology Department has given you an entire wing, and this is how you thank them?"

She stares at me in disbelief.

"They don't talk, P," I say, backtracking. "Animals don't talk. And you're a respected scientist, not Dr. Doolittle."

"You're threatened by me," she says.

"Oh, come on. What is that supposed to—"

"That's why you never read my papers." She backs against the bureau, nodding. "That's why you want me to turn down the fellowship."

The stint in Germany, she means. Of all times, she raises it now? "Don't change the subject," I say. "That has nothing to—"

"And that's why you were late to my speech."

"I wasn't late."

"And it's okay, isn't it? Because you happen to be the only animal on earth that thinks and feels. Am I right?"

"Are you drunk?"

Her nostrils flare. As she turns away from me, the image of Frank holding Rex rears up before me, and I feel a dull pang of remorse.

"P . . ." She has yanked open the top drawer of the dresser, rooting for something.

"You said we should get your dad on lithium," I say. "Well,

your speech wasn't all that different from his. If you're so concerned about animal welfare, why aren't you a vegetarian?" I try to catch her eye in the mirror, but her face is in shadow.

"And if you really do believe they have thoughts," I continue, "propose a way to show that empirically. Don't just accuse your colleagues of anthropocentrism."

"Thoughts don't necessarily correspond to behavior," she mutters. "That's the point."

She is ransacking the drawer that holds everything and nothing: glue, brochures, May's broken kite, things for holding other things together. As a coupon for a frequent flyer program floats to the rug, I suddenly remember the Galápagos tickets I had planned to surprise her with tonight, and feel a surge of reproach and melancholy.

"We can rehash behaviorism another day," I say. "But translating birdsong into English? That's insane."

She says nothing. The only sound is the shuffle of junk.

"Even if we agree to call their vocalizations 'language' someday," I continue, "there's no compelling evidence that animals are doing anything beyond protecting territory, jousting for mates, courting them, and so on. Claiming that they have ideas—I mean, my god, that's the height of anthropomorphism. Narcissism, as you put it. That's exactly the kind of assumption you were *criticizing*."

When she does not reply I add, although the fact is self-evident, "They're not epistemic subjects, P."

"*Epistemic subjects*." She wheels around, comb in hand. "Can you speak like a normal person for once?"

"It's shorthand," I say, swallowing the insult. "They don't reason. They don't feel shame. I mean, Jesus, I can't believe I have to say these things aloud."

"You know what I love?" she says. "I love that your criterion of what constitutes a thinking being is a phrase almost none of them has heard."

"It's just shorthand," I repeat, when she turns back to the mirror. "You know what I mean."

"Of course." She yanks a knot out of her hair. "Sorry, I forgot. You're a fucking logical positivist. Language is failed mathematics. Pardon me."

"I admire the positivists," I say, surprised. "I don't affiliate with any movement."

She breaks out in ugly laughter. I draw my knees up to my chest, my heart racing.

"Okay, I'm done." She drops the comb back in the dresser, closing the drawer so forcefully that the mirror rattles. "I'm wrong. You're right. You win."

She flings open the linen closet and eases a duvet from the upper shelf. With a bolt of desperation, I realize she is planning to sleep elsewhere—in the living room, presumably—which she has never done before.

"I'm just confused," I say. "You caught me so off guard, today. You're not a philosopher. You're not a critical theorist. You're a very distinguished scientist, and your work has nothing to do with—"

"Oh, don't pretend you give a shit about my work."

I swallow, steadying myself.

"It's wonky," she continues, "simplistic, naïve . . . *Animal language*"—her voice plummets, mimicking mine—"my, how *contradictory.*"

"Well, guilty as charged, Prue." I open my arms, relieved to finally say it. "This stuff is kind of batty. It's not serious. It's not you."

"So testing for intelligence is serious, and testing for language is pseudoscience?" She clutches the blanket to her chest. "I don't get it, Ivan. I don't see the difference."

"There's a world of difference," I say, incredulous. She must be delusional. "A *world* of difference—literally—between puzzle solving and language. *This*"—I gesture between us—"they don't do this."

"I would hope not."

She flings the blanket on the bed. Tugging out the wrinkles, she adds, "I'll stick to puzzle solving, then. Would that make you feel better?"

"I don't think you should stick to anything, I just . . . ," I trail off, talked into a corner.

With a savage laugh, she says, "Don't get me wrong. I don't mind your disapproval. Sometimes it even excites me. *She'll pay a price,* you were probably thinking all night. *That bad girl.*"

I am silent. We have tumbled ahead, into new territory. A murderous freedom is in the air.

"What?" She straightens, flushed. "Too much for you?"

She is breathing with an almost comic intensity. I have a sudden, terrible urge to laugh.

"No, it's just . . ." I bite my lip. "Don't make this about sex, P."

"Funny you should say that, because I think sex is just about the only thing we have going for us anymore."

"You don't mean that," I say quietly. "Don't say things you don't—"

"Why are you still sitting here?" she interrupts. "Go"—she gestures at the corridor—"read some more of my email, why don't you, or better yet, gorge yourself on my food."

This is a fresh blow, unprecedented. Heat rushes into my face.

"Now that I think about it," she says, "I bet you wanted my dad to hurt Rex."

"*What?*" My ears ring. She is talking nonsense now.

"That's why you stood back and let him mortify me in front of everyone."

"Listen to yourself. You sound crazier than your father."

"You wanted something bad to happen," she says, nodding. "You wanted me to pay. And all for taking one *fucking* risk."

She stares at me, astonished. There are tears in her eyes, yet she seems about to laugh.

"How could I not have seen it?" Her voice breaks. "Your passive aggression is the bravest thing about you."

"Are you finished?" I roar.

A sob leaves her.

In silence I stride into the bathroom and brush my teeth. When I return she has curled up under the two duvets, her face obscured.

"I don't get it," I say.

She doesn't answer. I suddenly wish I were alone with my anger, and will her to storm out of the bedroom after all.

"You're up for tenure," I say. "We have a life here."

Her breath catches.

"And you're willing to throw it all away?"

"Please stop talking," she whispers.

I crawl under the quilt, keeping close to the edge. She is still crying, but softly. After a while her breathing levels out, and then she flops onto her side, abruptly, with the wild candor of sleep.

My heart is still pounding. To temper it I synchronize my breaths to hers. A smoke alarm goes off in the distance, and then subsides. Whether an hour has passed, or less, I cannot tell.

"P?" I say, into the darkness.

The sound hangs in the air. Then it fades, until I might as well have said nothing.

Ten

I have always envied Prue's ability to sleep through anything. I don't know how she does it. Not even thunder wakes her, whereas almost any sound, no matter how innocent, will pitch me back into the world.

So it is only natural that the cough of our Subaru should rouse me, despite the indecent hour—1:52, the clock declares, in mean red numerals—and the insulated wall that separates our room from the driveway.

I scramble out of bed. Reaching the kitchen and stuffing my feet into my boots, I wonder dimly whether I dreamed the sound. But when I burst out into the cold the car is idling there, its taillights burning. Snow falls through the cones of orange light. As I jog forward it starts again with a ragged aspiration, jolting toward the darkened road.

"Stop!" I call out.

It accelerates. I stoop to gather something, anything, to throw at the rear windshield, and instead jam my fingers into ice. Knuckles throbbing, I stamp the ground with my heel and dislodge a wedge of snow, hurling it at the retreating fender. There is a gentle thump. The car slows. I throw another wedge and miss, just as the front wheels clear the driveway and begin to turn. In the illuminated cabin I catch a glimpse of two wrinkled hands on the steering wheel. Desperate, I break into a run, cursing myself for failing to hide the keys.

He is driving faster now. Still running, I bend—hopping twice—and fling my boot. It hits the side mirror, and the car lurches to a stop.

"God damn it, Frank," I pant, when he opens the side window. "Where are you going?"

"Noboru's." He gestures ahead, his breath coming in clouds.

"Noboru *Hayashi's*?"

He nods. "Fourteen Willoughby Lane. Right around the corner."

Melting snow burns through my sock. I say, "Get out of the car."

"I'm already—"

"*Out.*"

He casts a supplicating look in my direction, and then relents, stepping out into the cold. As I retrieve my boot and park the car he waits by the side of the road, brooding. Not until we have entered the kitchen does he speak again.

"If you'd have let me, I could have straightened things out."

He is wearing the suit he wore yesterday, his checkered tie clipped, the cuffs of his shirt neatly folded. His suede loafers are damp. The outsoles are blotched, probably ruined, rimmed with spurs of translucent snow.

"I fucked up earlier," he adds. He must have showered, because his wet hair is brushed back. The scratch on his jaw has faded to a dark pink line.

"What . . ." I shake my head, at a loss. "What does Noboru Hayashi have to do with anything?"

Frank frowns. "Thought he was the chair of Biology."

"And?"

"Please don't mention this to Prue." He pinches the bridge of his nose, blinking fiercely. "Look, I know I went overboard today. I . . ."—he closes his eyes—"I tried to do it by phone, but he wouldn't hear me out."

I snatch up our landline and scroll through the dialed calls. Three appear, placed ten minutes ago to the same local number.

"Jesus, Frank."

"I get it." He nods. "I moved too quickly for those folks. I'm no rhetorician, like she is."

"How on earth did you get his information?"

"Nothing's private these days." He gestures toward Prue's laptop, still sleeping on the counter. "Now if you'd let me at the car, I—"

"So you can get yourself arrested?"

"So I can apologize, all right? Convince him that what happened had nothing to do with Prue, with . . ." He rubs his neck. "I'm not an idiot. I know the guy has a lot of say in her tenure case."

I peel off my wet sock and drape it over the radiator. "It doesn't work like that, Frank. Tenure happens by vote. The 'chair' title isn't even an honorific. It just saddles you with more committee work."

"But—"

"Besides," I interrupt, putting a length of countertop between us. "You can't impact your daughter's tenure prospects, Frank. Sorry to break it to you, but you don't have that power."

"But you said he wouldn't want anything more to do with Prue. Him and the rest of them, after what I—"

"No, Frank. After what *she* did." When he narrows his eyes I add, swamped by the memory, "After that lecture she gave."

"You don't look good, kid," he says.

"Well, it's two o'clock in the morning, Frank, and you just hijacked our car."

Pipes shudder in the wall. I can't help muttering, into his silence, "You do realize what Prue did."

He waits, studying me.

"Using her platform to moralize like that? Insult her colleagues . . ." The words ring hollow, somehow. I comb my fingers through my hair, trying to drum up the indignation I felt yesterday. "She blew it, Frank. You had nothing to do with it."

He says softly, "You understood."

There is a familiar gleam in his eye. As he speaks again I remember our fiasco in the diner, and then his provocation: *Entitled to some privacy, aren't I?*

"You get it," he says, as though to himself. "You know it's true, deep down—what she said. That's why it's killing you."

He looks so pathetic standing there, spouting nonsense in his cheap, stained suit, that I almost pity him.

"Have you taken your meds today?" I say quietly.

"That's why you blew up at her."

My stomach drops. When he does not elaborate I say, carefully, "When?"

"When." He guffaws. "A few hours ago is when. Shouting at her, after all she'd accomplished."

The injustice of the comment seethes through me like a cramp. I cannot listen to this—not now, not ever again.

"You're lucky you're not in jail right now, Frank," I say. "If I hadn't woken up—"

"It was nice to hear you let loose, honestly." His eyes sparkle. "Didn't know you had it in you."

Without another word I storm down the hall and into the guest room, flicking the light on and sifting through his duffel bag. No pill bottle. I am about to check the bathroom for it when my eyes snag on an orange glow. The vial is perched on the shelf, between a dictionary and one of May's stuffed bears.

When I return to the kitchen Frank has lowered himself onto a stool, regarding me pensively. His gaze does not waver as I approach him, holding out the vial.

"You've been lying about these, haven't you?" I say.

He chuckles wryly. As I press down the thick white cap and twist, a look of weariness crosses his face.

"Would you like some food with it?"

He glances from me to the vial and back. A starchy smell issues from the rim, then fades.

"Do it for your daughter, Frank," I say.

He opens his palm. Hastily, I shake out one pale green pill, about to offer him some water when he knocks it back.

"Thank you," I say, as he swallows.

He nods, and then stands up.

"You're sure you don't want anything to eat?"

"I'm good. Sorry for waking you."

In silence he limps down the corridor. Then he disappears into his room.

I lean against the wall, drawing four deep breaths. The house is quiet. Behind the drone of the refrigerator comes a whirring sound, punctuated by irregular clicks: the heater, or some other domestic artery.

I should feel relieved. But without Frank to distract me, the dam I have erected against the memory of last night's savagery—my accusations, Prue's retorts—begins to weaken. To reinforce it I return to the kitchen and burn through a bag of tortilla chips, thinking of Noboru. No point in calling him back now, or perhaps tomorrow, either. He may not have even recognized Frank's voice. And if he has, the damage is done.

On my way back to bed I lean into the study to check on May. Prue left the door wide open, partly for her sake and partly so that Rex can fly back when he pleases. May is curled up near the edge of the mattress, the moonlight blanching her hair.

She lifts her head. "Grandpa?"

"It's me, honey."

She rolls over, pushing her bangs out of her eyes. "I heard Grandpa."

"He couldn't sleep. But he's back in bed now."

I lower myself onto the mattress, inadvertently crushing her hand, which slithers free.

She whispers, "I had a bad dream."

Frank prides himself on scaring off May's nightmares. When they multiplied during Walt's divorce, he instructed Walt to tape his number to the wall beside her bed so she could call him whenever she woke up. From his attic room up north—nearly every night, we later learned—he would take her call and lull her back to sleep.

THE STUDY OF ANIMAL LANGUAGES

"What happened?" I say, but she only shakes her head.

When I squeeze her hand to comfort her, she says, "Can you tell me a story?"

"A story?" I lean forward, propping my elbows on my knees. "I don't know if I've got one, May."

"Like one of Grandpa's."

"Let's see . . ."

As I wrack my brain, she snuggles up to her favorite stuffed animal—a penguin she has christened Maurice.

"Once upon a time there was a spy," I say at last. "She knew everything about everyone, except—"

"Is it true, what he said about boiled bones?" she interrupts.

"What who said?"

"Grandpa." She fingers Maurice's cotton beak. "About boiled bones and hearts and skin? In all our stuff?"

"No, it wasn't true," I say, surprised to feel a flicker of guilt at lying, or half-lying, to her.

"So why did he say it?"

"He was confused." I tuck her hair behind her ear, my guilt yielding to indignation. If Frank really cares about animal products—and he had probably exaggerated their pervasiveness—he should join PETA.

I say, "He's sick, sweetheart."

"Does he have a temperature?"

"It's his thoughts." I tap my forehead. "He gets scary thoughts, sometimes, that tell him to do scary things."

"When's he going to get better?"

"Soon. I promise."

She closes her eyes. I wait until she has fallen asleep, then tuck the quilt around her. Gradually I stand up, wincing as the springs creak.

She doesn't stir. But when I reach the door she says, "Uncle Ivan?"

"Yes?"

The mound of blankets shifts.

"What about his real thoughts?"

"Whose?"

"Grandpa's."

"They're there," I say. "They'll be there."

The aviary looms over her body, in partial shadow. A complicated darkness on the upper perch confirms that Rex has returned to the cage.

Eleven

———

When I wake up it is after eleven, and I'm alone. Light gushes across the duvet. *Damn,* Walt has texted me. *Thought we'd seen the worst of him.* Prue must have filled him in on yesterday's ordeal. One of them, at least. Without replying I swing my feet out of bed, my gut flaming from last night's chips.

As I leave the bedroom, freshly showered, the Looney Tunes opening glissando filters from the living room. The house smells different—heavier, somehow—and as I move down the corridor the scent intensifies. When I reach the living room, where May and Frank are perched before Prue's laptop, I discover its source: an ocean of flowers—asphodel, gladioli, hydrangeas, and more, spilling from ceramic pots that cover every free surface. There are easily two dozen, each one bearing a tiny paper card.

"Clichéd, I know," Frank says, from the couch. "But it was the most I could do last minute."

I open one of the cards. "Sorry" it reads. So does the next one. And the next.

"She didn't even see them, though." He scratches his head. "Ordered them last night, express, but she left before they got here."

"How much did you spend on all this?" I say, as May giggles.

"Not as much as I deserve."

She tugs his sleeve, pointing at the screen. They must have reconciled, somehow. Before them, Sylvester resuscitates a wheezing Porky Pig.

There are more flowers in the kitchen, resting on stools, the table, and even—precariously—the radio. Frank must have blown at least three hundred dollars. I transfer the radio bouquet to the countertop and set a pot of water on high heat, my stomach roiled by the mismatched fragrances. Outside, the road has been plowed, the lawns and roofs gleaming with snow. The sky is a furious blue.

I wake my phone and touch Prue's name. She answers right away.

"I'm at the lab," she says. Our car is still outside, so she must have walked. She adds, "Had to tie a few things up."

The thickness in her voice tells me that she has been waiting for my call. We rarely fight, and when we do, we never go to sleep without resolving things. I am usually the first to capitulate.

"May seems okay," I say, stalling.

She sighs. "I tried the number for my dad's old psychiatrist, but she didn't pick up. I don't know if he's even seeing her anymore."

I take a breath, about to tell her about the flowers, and then exhale. If anything, they should have come from me.

She says, "He seemed okay this morning."

We'll get past this, her tone says. The water twitches in the pot. As she starts to speak again, I rehearse this evening's reunion in my mind. She will have spent the day out, nursing her grievances, and when she returns I will have handled dinner. We will both be especially mild with one another, mutually intent on inserting a buffer of time and care between ourselves and our recriminations.

". . . guess an aquatic zoo is off the table after yesterday," she concludes. "Hello?"

"I'm here." I drop an egg into the pot, setting the timer to seven minutes. "Look, P . . ." I lean against the counter. "Let me handle things today. I'll get them out of the house, somehow. We'll bring back food."

There is a scuffling in the background, and then a voice I cannot place.

"P?" I say.

"Yes, I heard you. That sounds fine."

"I'm sorry about last night."

She doesn't answer. She is in no mood to rehash things now, her silence implies, but I repeat myself anyhow, adding, "I'd had a lot to drink."

Another stillness. I check the phone, only to find it has run out of battery. My voice echoes in my ears—foreign, somehow—belonging to the version of myself I am to her. I plug the phone back in, waiting the requisite few minutes for it to revive itself. When I call back, she doesn't pick up.

"What do you say we get you a haircut?" I suggest, sliding onto the couch beside May and Frank. He is paging through a copy of *The Nation* he must have brought from home.

May ignores me, riveted to the screen, where a fleet of mice—armed with machetes—are marching toward a sleeping cat.

"I don't think the aquarium's open today," I lie. "But there are plenty of other things we can—"

"What?" She turns to me, incredulous, as the mice attack. "But you *said*. I promised Maurice."

Her stuffed penguin, she means. He is nestled on her lap, bedecked in the sweater Frank sewed him last Christmas. May is wearing her favorite red overalls which, I realize, with a sinking heart, she must have put on specially for the outing. Her battered notebook protrudes from the front pocket.

"You *said*," she repeats. At the note of panic in her voice Frank looks up.

"What is it, bug?" He peers over his reading glasses.

"The aquarium's closed," she says, her voice rising, as the animated cat pleads for mercy.

"Not closed, necessarily," I break in. "Just—"

"It's Saturday," Frank interrupts. "What kind of balderdash is that?"

"The aquarium." I catch his eye, asking, silently, *Can you handle this?*

The egg timer beeps from the kitchen. As May whispers some reassurance into the place where the penguin's ear would be, Frank reaches out and pats my hand.

"We'll storm it, if necessary," he says, returning to his magazine. "Hear that, Maurice?"

THE AQUARIUM is a twenty-minute drive from our house, on the site of a former sardine cannery. A winged structure with an aluminum façade, it overlooks the southern stretch of Narragansett Bay, and hosts a snorkeling camp May attended last summer.

Since we moved here it has tripled in size, transforming a formerly barren plaza into a bustling promenade.

The radio predicted hail, so despite the confident blue sky I armed us with three umbrellas, including a windproof, steel number Prue bought after losing one of mine. Frank—still unsteady on his twisted knee—elects to use it as a cane, swinging it affably through the fluted glass archway.

The place is crowded for the season. Babysitters in galoshes float up the central escalator, while bovine fathers linger at the popcorn stand. "Share the Wonder," a poster commands, pointing the way toward an exhibit on cephalopods. A fiberglass orca hangs from the ceiling, its belly dull with fingerprints. Beneath it is a large, magenta jungle gym, shaped like an anemone. May bolts for it while I join the ticket line, shoving Maurice into Frank's arms.

"This place is a joke," he says when I return.

I glance sharply at May, who is skipping back toward us, and then back at him. He grunts, fixing the adhesive ticket to his shirt.

As we mount the escalator, however, I cannot help but see his point. The place feels tawdrier than I remember, more like a theme park—with its loud decor and cheerless employees—than a conservation initiative.

On the landing a blond man intercepts us, pushing a mobile stand.

"Fancy an audio guide?" he says.

Frank refuses, but I rent one for May. The man briefs me, jauntily, on the numeric keypad. He has a gelled coiffure and an Australian accent.

"Rockhoppers are getting peckish." He grins. "Don't miss their feeding. Twenty minutes from now, across from Open Sea."

"That means you," May whispers to Maurice. She beams at the man, then says, with adult grace, "Thank you, sir."

We enter the mouth of the main exhibit, a tunnel lined with towering photographs and mirrors warped to resemble waves. A black-and-white anemone looms at the other end, its tentacles so intricate that it takes me a moment to realize they are painted, a hoax of chiaroscuro. Two men and a child rear up before us, the older man amplified by a pucker in the glass, the other telescoped. Only when the child points ahead, in time with May, do I recognize us.

"Sandy shore!" she exclaims. "Our counselors took us here!"

She drags us toward a touching tank affixed to the far wall. Children swarm around it, dunking their hands into the shallow water. As May elbows her way between them a girl raises her dripping hands, brandishing a sea cucumber. She aims it at the boy beside her, glancing furtively at the attendant as she squeezes the creature, which emits a plume of clear liquid. The boy shrieks. I turn to Frank, expecting a scowl, but he is taking in the neighboring exhibit, which features shoreline birds. An egret is poised behind the glass, scratching its cheek with one long toe. Its curated beach stretches about five yards, lengthened by a painted river. An artificial creek undulates between the boulders, extending almost seamlessly into the image.

Two small birds—plovers, according to the supplementary text—emerge from behind the farthest boulder. One of them cocks its speckled head, facing us, as the other nudges a pebble with its beak. The egret paces the length of the glass, each step like an umbrella closing.

"Are you all right?" I murmur.

"Fine," Frank says. His eyes are bloodshot. Between the car debacle and ordering all those flowers, he can't have slept much.

"You let me know if you'd rather meet us in the gift shop, okay?" I say.

Instead of replying he jabs a button on my audio guide, and a silvery voice peals through it: "Welcome to the Rhode Island Aquarium. Home to some of the world's most unforgettable marine life. Radiant reptiles. Cunning crustaceans. Flashy fish. Whoever you are, we have something for you. Thank you for choosing . . ."

Frank says, "Goddamn tentacles are tangled."

He gestures at a tank across the room, featuring a cluster of striped pink jellyfish, some of them intertwined.

"They're probably mating, or something," I say, turning off the machine.

"Place doesn't strike me as a turn-on." He sniffs, then wipes his nose with his sleeve. He is wearing one of his habitual outfits: a dark blue flannel shirt tucked into corduroys. Before we left, I had taken the liberty of removing the pens from his breast pocket. The move seemed priggish in retrospect, given his display of contrition this morning. But that seems to be flagging now.

"Let's just get to the penguins, okay, Frank?" I say. "Then we'll be out of here."

Keeping one eye on him, I turn back toward the touching tank, laying a hand on May's shoulder.

"Sweetie? Let's move on. We don't want to miss . . ."

The girl who turns to face me is not May. She has a fragile, Irish face, and her bright red overalls are velvet, rather than stained denim. There is a mollusk in her hand.

"Sorry." I step back.

"Ow!" she shrieks. What I took for a snail is a hermit crab, and it has pinched her. She drops it on the ground, prompting a squeal of horror from the boy beside her. I catch it as it skitters between my ankles, then plop it back into the water.

"May?" I call out, my mouth dry.

A stroller wheel rolls over my foot. Had she wandered back to the entry tunnel? No. The only people over there are a squat, elderly man and a teenage couple. Around me, the noises of the crowd resound with fresh barbarity. "We don't know for sure why mobula rays leap," a young man says, addressing a throng of children in green shirts, "but some scientists think they find it fun." A lone ray sweeps across the glass behind him, wings listing. From the mouth of the next exhibit comes another dark-haired girl who is not May.

"Wait here," I tell Frank, and circle the touching tank, calling, and then shouting May's name.

A few adults glance my way, alarmed. Family units glide past. The young man has finished his speech; the green-shirted children are turning toward me as one. With savage clarity, I see it: the intercom announcement, the troubled strangers, the return to the car without May.

"Excuse me," I say to the attendant stationed at the touching tank. "Have you . . ." I swallow, trying to moisten my parched throat. "Have you seen a girl with dark brown hair and glasses, seven years old?"

"Just a moment." She turns toward a child whose features might as well be blank. "Keep your hand flat, that's right. . . ."

With outrageous care, she lays a glistening starfish across his palm.

"Ma'am, please." I touch her arm. "I need your help."

And then they are upon me. May is chattering, yanking me toward the next exhibit, while Frank stares down into the tank.

"Where have you *been*?" I say, flooded with calm and jubilant indignation.

"It's the chameleon fish!" she exclaims. "Maurice found it. Come on!"

I catch her free hand as she skips ahead, unwilling to lose physical contact. The next exhibit is considerably darker, crowned by a neon sign that reads "Magicians of the Deep." The progression comes back to me, vaguely, from a visit years ago. Here is the exhibit on cephalopods, followed by the penguin habitat.

"Where was she?" I ask Frank, but he doesn't answer. He whisks his forefingers over his eyebrows, then bends to inspect a paper nautilus. Around us, bioluminescent squid shimmer in the walls.

May pulls me toward a cubic tank, which appears to host nothing but seaweed. It convulses, obeying some hidden current, and then the fronds part to reveal an orange mass with the texture of scrambled eggs. To its left, mounted above a touchscreen, moon jellies throb in synchrony.

"A movie!" May says. She prods the screen to life.

"The cuttlefish is nature's hypnotist," says a jocular, male voice. "Check out its powers of camouflage, which make this critter an expert at wooing mates."

A coral reef appears, patrolled by schools of minnows. All at once, a patch of it resolves into a purplish shape. The creature dips its narrow snout, ruffles its fins. Then the rocks and minnows reassert themselves.

"There he is," May whispers to Maurice, indicating the tank before us.

The same purplish body drifts across the sand. When it turns its leathered face in our direction, I feel as though I am gazing across millennia of evolutionary change.

For perhaps the first time, as I am meeting—or failing to meet—its gibbous eyes, I feel the lunacy of Darwin's vision. The animal might as well be extraterrestrial. That we could share an ancestor, however protozoan, strikes me as so preposterous that I laugh.

Frank has caught up to us. He murmurs, "Are you getting this?"

His eyes glitter. They dart to the tank of moon jellies, then to the next exhibit, where bands of light—refracted through a tank so huge I can make out only part of it, from here—are rippling across the floor.

"Getting what, Frank?"

"They're . . . ," he trails off, distracted by the cuttlefish. His eyes widen. With a shaking hand, he grabs my wrist.

"What is it, Frank?" I say, as May babbles to Maurice. "What's going on?"

Frank presses his finger to his lips. Then he raises it in the air, as I have seen him do outside, to test the direction of the wind.

A male voice booms from the loudspeaker: "Good afternoon, folks. Just a friendly reminder that our penguin feeding will begin in *fi-i-ve*"—his voice dips—"minutes! Head on over to the Flipper Zone to see our rockhoppers chow down."

May scurries toward the next room. I start to pull Frank toward her, but he drops my wrist. He is still staring at the cuttlefish.

I reach for him, but he steps back. Then he says, in a strange, clear voice, "No, it's not your fault."

My chest tightens. A boy on a leash toddles past us, wailing, his mother in tow.

"Come on!" May calls from the threshold. Then she scampers out of sight.

I seize Frank's elbow and haul him after her.

"It's ours," he mumbles. "We did this."

He is talking to the fish, no doubt. Idiocy, to take him here. Swearing under my breath, I spot May up ahead, standing on her tiptoes to see over the crowd. The penguin tank rises before her.

Sunlight pours through it. After the dimness of the last room I have to squint as we approach the staggered cliff, encircled by smudged glass. The penguins are standing side by side on a lower ledge. I can just make out their strong, pinched faces, their plumed eyebrows. Most of them are honking, fins raised, like bickering commissars. For creatures going nowhere they move with enviable purpose.

"We've gotta go, sweetie," I say, when we reach her.

May stares at me in disbelief.

"Grandpa's not feeling well."

"But they're about to eat!"

A uniformed woman has appeared on the cliff, carrying a bullhorn and green bucket. The people around us push forward, jockeying for a better view, as the penguins bluster off their ledge.

"Pipe down a second," Frank calls out—to the penguins, I realize, with horror. As he lifts his finger again I step between him and May, trawling my mind for a plan.

"Don't worry, we'll get you something even better later," she says to Maurice, lifting him over her head for a better view.

"My god," Frank says, staring over my shoulder at the adjacent exhibit. "It can't be. They can't have . . ."

I turn to find a slice of ocean, girded by a pane of glass so tall I have to step back to take it in. "Welcome to Open Sea," reads an overhanging poster. Vast, green structures sway behind it, interposed by flashing schools of herring. Before us, two hammerhead sharks glide in tandem. One of their mouths hangs open, revealing an arsenal of pointed teeth.

Frank strides toward them, nearly tripping over a stroller. To my relief, the exhibit is more or less deserted, eclipsed by the penguin feeding. Perhaps he'll take it in without bothering anyone. But no—he is flagging down an employee now, who approaches him cheerfully. I aim for them, grabbing May's hand.

"Hey." May strains against me.

"I'm sorry, honey, but we have to stay with Grandpa."

"They're not done yet," she whines, stumbling after me.

"Let's go get him. He can't miss this!"

Frank is gesticulating to the attendant, dwarfed by the kelp forest. Against its majesty his gestures look skittish, puerile. For a moment I allow myself to imagine him as someone else's charge, a stranger whom, in some other—equally plausible—life, I never would have met.

"... only hold the white sharks for a few months," the attendant says, as we approach. "And then we release them."

Whatever Frank says next prompts her to stifle a grin. She can't be much older than twenty, but there is an air of authority about her. Her hair is plaited in sleek cornrows.

"Castration?" she says. "Do you mean surgical neutering, sir?" He nods fiercely. "No, we definitely don't do that. These animals are close to endangered. If anything, we want them to breed in captivity so we don't have to collect them from the wild."

May must have sensed that something is wrong, because she has stopped protesting. She shrinks against me.

"What gives you the right to collect them at all?" Frank says, and the attendant glances at me, alarmed.

"I'm so sorry." I lay a hand on Frank's arm. "You'll have to excuse him. He doesn't realize what he's saying."

Two people nearby are eyeing us now. Something like schadenfreude flickers between them. I marvel, as I have before, at how easily anger can reorganize a room. One rupture in civility, and attention rushes toward it, predictably as matter toward a void.

To my surprise, the attendant smiles. "I get it," she says. "It's a common misconception people have about aquariums—that we harm the animals, or neglect them, like they used to do in zoos. But that's not true, at least nowadays. We're about habitats, not cages." She turns to Frank. "And, sir, I can tell you that inspiring conservation isn't just our priority. It's our mission."

A cry of wonder rises from the penguin exhibit, followed by

a splash. The voice on the loudspeaker mutters something that elicits scattered, adult laughter.

"So diminished," Frank whispers, as a shark cruises past us. With a twinge of embarrassment, I see him as he must appear to her, with his wild hair and faded clothes and bright old eyes, wet with grief and passion.

"Are you folks from around here?" she asks me. Then she jumps, startled, as Frank stabs the floor with the ferrule of his umbrella.

"Take them home," he barks at her. May's hand closes around my thumb.

"Let's go," I hiss, grabbing Frank's arm. To the attendant, I say: "Thanks for your time. I really do apologize."

Frank wrenches free, then shoves me back with surprising force. I stumble against May, who has begun to cry.

"Let them *out*," he bellows.

There is nothing familiar in his expression. He clutches the tapered end of his umbrella, raising its steel handle in the air. The attendant gasps.

"Don't!" I shout, but he is already in motion. I dive for May as, in one agile sweep, he swings the metal toward the glass.

Twelve

I see the impact before it comes: the crash, the rushing water, the sleek gray bodies lunging at us between splinters of glass. The force of the image drives me against May, pushing her down to shield her from the wreckage. She screams, and before I can explain, the stone floor races up to meet us. Then comes the fragile crunch of her glasses against my cheek, the twinkle of pain.

A tinny flavor enters my mouth. May is crushed beneath me, straining for air. There are shouts, running footsteps. When I roll off her and lift my face, however, I see no carnage. The same beasts are gliding overhead, with ancient poise. Before them, staring stunned at the bull's-eye crack he has inflicted, is an old man wielding an umbrella.

By the time I have scrambled to my feet they are upon him. A uniformed man grabs him by the shoulders, steering him through a camouflaged door beside the tank. Another employee stands in the threshold of the cephalopod exhibit, barking into a radio. Behind us, the penguin feeding continues, though most of the onlookers have turned to stare. Some of them are hurrying toward the next hall, clutching purses and toddlers to their chest. The attendant we were speaking to has disappeared.

May is crawling across the floor, groping for something. Her glasses are splayed on the stone behind her, one lens shattered. In some cosmic gesture of sympathy, they must have fallen off her face before breaking against mine.

"Hi there, folks." The same male voice that had announced the penguin feeding blasts through the hall: "We regret to announce that our rockhopper exhibit is temporarily closed, I repeat, closed. If you are in the area, please find the nearest exit. We should have this cleared up momentarily."

I lift May up and carry her toward the camouflaged door where they have taken Frank. She is whimpering, but seems physically unhurt. Just as we reach the door, it swings open, revealing a bearded attendant.

"Please stay back, sir," he says.

"That man in there . . ." I gesture toward the fluorescent hallway behind him. "He's with us."

"Authorized staff only."

His gaze lingers on my cheek, and I reach up to feel a jagged stickiness. My fingers come away bloody.

Two personnel in navy suits push past us, clutching their radios. The man nods, beckoning them inside. And then the door shuts.

May is shaking all over. I hold her close to me and scan the room, wondering whether we should return to the lobby. A clearing has opened up before the tank, ringed by five staff members with clipboards. The crack is about the size of a tennis ball, a network of shrill white rays that impose a Euclidean violence on the water.

I am about to approach the staff members when a police officer sidles past us, through the camouflaged door. As it hisses closed on its mechanical arm I stick my foot in the threshold, waiting a few seconds. Then I slip inside.

"Where are we going?" May says.

I hold a finger to my lips, and she nods.

We follow the officer down a corridor paved with lime green carpeting. There are doors on either side of us, distinguished by copper nameplates. Parabolic lamps buzz overhead.

The officer takes a left and disappears. Shifting May onto my other hip, I hurry after him, rounding a corner into a hall that opens out into a glassed-in conference room. Three people are blocking the entrance, murmuring to one another. Others are clustered inside, around an oblong table. Between a pair of shifting bodies I catch a glimpse of Frank. He is sitting with his back to us, nearly swallowed by an ergonomic chair. The employees are staring at him with a mixture of disgust and fascination. From where we stand I can make out a few of their muttered phrases: ". . . evacuation . . . till Lisa paged me . . . that old guy? . . ." They fall silent as the officer approaches.

"Him," says a woman in black, pointing at Frank. Her jacket reads "Security." As the officer moves toward him, her eyes settle on me and May.

"Can I help you, sir?" she says sharply.

"I'm here to collect that man." I gesture toward the conference room. "He's my—"

"Who gave you access to this area?"

"No one. I . . . Wait"—she is speaking into her radio now—
"He's not well. He's been off his medication."

Some of her colleagues have noticed us, too. She hesitates. In
their collective gaze I sense the same revulsion they had directed
at Frank, and it plants a foreign desperation in my voice.

"He's bipolar," I blurt out, feeling May's breath quicken
against my collarbone. "If you'll just let me through . . . "

"The police are handling the situation, sir. You can meet him
at the precinct."

Inside the conference room I notice the Australian man.
Somehow, through everything, I have managed to keep hold of
my audio guide.

On impulse I shout, "Frank!"

He turns, and our eyes meet. I see terror in his face, muddied
by confusion. And then the police officer steps between us.

"Sir?" the woman is saying now. "If you don't cooperate, I'm
afraid we're going to have to escort you out of the building."

The prospect of ceding Frank to the state—and having to
confess as much to Prue—fills me with dread.

"But, the meds . . . He needs them now," I say—pure
invention—yet I am suddenly willing to stake my life on the lie.
"This has happened before, I'm telling you. Please. I have them
on me."

She is no longer listening. One of her colleagues steps forward, and together they steer me and May into a back stairwell,
guiding us down two empty flights. By the time we have reached
the ground floor, I have extracted Frank's destination: the Narragansett Police Department, on Wanda Drive.

"Someone should take a look at your face," the woman says in parting, taking my audio guide and pushing open a barred door marked Exit.

Rain slams against us. I push back against the door, my arms aching from May's weight, only to find that it is locked from within. I am standing between a loading dock and a garage, facing a welter of cars that bear no resemblance to the tidy lot we entered an hour ago. A siren howls. People scamper toward their SUVs, some of them holding plastic bags over their heads.

When I lower May to the ground, she sucks in her breath. A few strands of hair are sticking to her tearstained cheek. She stares with horror at mine.

I bring my hand to the wound and feel a viscid warmth. The blood must be running under the freezing rain. I start to explain as much, but she is already tugging off Maurice's sweater, balling it up and pressing it against my cheek. Too surprised to thank her, I tug her hood over her head and lead her out across the pavement.

"Listen for it," I tell her, pressing the panic button on the electronic key fob.

Our car is mercifully close. So is the police station, I find, once we climb in and I have Googled the address. I pull out of our parking space, flicking the windshield wipers on high.

"You said he was getting better," May whimpers.

Lightning flashes in the distance. They must have evacuated the place, because the entrance to the highway is jammed.

"I know, honey. I'm sorry."

"Everything's blurry."

"We'll get you new glasses."

A thunderclap prompts her to cry out. As we finally pull onto the highway she whispers, "I want to go home."

"That's where we're headed, just as soon as we pick up Grandpa."

"I don't want Grandpa."

Still pressing the sweater to my face, I glance in the rearview mirror. Her face has crumpled. With a spasm of guilt, I imagine how she will recount this day, when she is older: *The time my grandpa almost killed me and my uncle. And my uncle didn't stop him.*

I say, "We have to rescue him, sweetie, before—"

"I don't want to rescue him." She wipes her face with Maurice. "I don't want to see him ever again."

"May . . ."

"I want to go home," she says through a sob. "I want my dad."

In silence I redirect the GPS to Walt's apartment. The half-hour detour takes us through the outskirts of West Warwick, down scrubby, rain-swept roads. The houses lining Walt's street are vinyl, some of them flanked by motor homes. A chariot draped in Christmas lights flashes on one lawn, steered by a plastic Santa. A wooden reindeer rears before him, its sodden scarf thrashing in the wind.

May unbuckles her seat belt before her house is even in sight. When I pull into her driveway, she struggles with the door lock.

"It's going to be all right," I say, unlocking her door. The clouds flash. She doesn't bother to reply, stumbling out of the car and across the icy lawn.

Walt opens the door in a robe. Julia must be here, I remember suddenly, as May throws her arms around his waist.

"What's up, guys?" he says, and then does a double take, noticing my cheek.

"Jesus," he adds. "What happened, man?"

From deeper in the house comes the roar of a televised crowd, mingled with the scent of pancakes. Their orange cat, Felix, weaves around his shins, its fur gone matte with cold.

I mutter, "Nothing I couldn't have predicted."

"Where's my dad?"

"At the police station."

"You're kidding. Hell'd he do now?"

"I'll explain later," I say, and glance meaningfully at May, unwilling to make her relive it.

"Well, come inside." He looks over his shoulder. "Let me just—"

"It's fine," I interrupt, backing away. "I have to go."

"Come on. At least—"

"Grandpa's sorry," I say to May.

She turns her puffy face toward mine. They watch from the doorway as I start the engine and revive the windshield wipers, speeding back in the direction of the sea.

THE POLICE STATION is only ten minutes from the aquarium, a homely building skirted by dunes of graying snow. Inside I find no sign of Frank. There is a backlog in Patrol, the receptionist informs me, but yes, their records do indicate a Franklin Baum in custody. He should be in Central Booking now, getting processed for arraignment. No, it won't be possible to see him at this time. Charges against him will depend on the prosecutor's evaluation. Corporal Banks will provide more details. He is on a break but should be back shortly. Once again, Mr. Baum's bail amount has not been set. Yes, he may be held overnight.

I lower myself into one of the lobby's plastic seats, across from a rangy, toothless man and a woman playing Sudoku. A rottweiler dozes between them, its nose twitching. The man glances at my cheek, and then averts his eyes.

My phone rings. Prue. Walt must have called her. May would have told him everything and worse by now.

"Oh god, P . . . ," I begin, but my voice gives out. I count the squares on the linoleum, collecting myself.

"I just got off with Walt," she says, wind lashing her voice. Can she be walking home from campus in this weather?

"He said May could hardly talk, she was so upset," she continues. "He said you ran off without an explanation. What *happened?*"

"Your dad . . . ," I say, anchored by the sound of her. "He completely freaked out."

"Where are you?"

"Some police station." I knead my forehead.

"Oh my god."

"We were at the aquarium." I prop my elbows on my knees. "He started hallucinating. He thought the animals were talking to him, that he had to help them."

She is silent.

"You know our good umbrella?" I take a breath, hardly believing what I am about to say, even though I witnessed it myself. "He swung it against the shark tank."

The Sudoku player glances up at me. I close my eyes.

"Just text me what town you're in," Prue says. "I'm out already. I'll call a cab."

"No, don't come here," I say. *Don't see him like this.*

"Of course I'm coming. How much cash should I bring?"

An officer leans through the door beside reception. "Ivan Link?"

"Here!" I stand up. Into the phone I say, "I have to go. I'll call you back."

"Wait, just tell me—"

"I have everything under control."

As soon as I hang up my phone flares back to life, but I decline her call. I should have answered, I realize, sickened, as I follow the officer through the doorway. But the thought of recounting the snarl of events—and with them, my incompetence—is too much to bear.

"Corporal B-banks'll see you now," the officer says, over her shoulder. "He'll answer any qu-questions you might have."

I follow her down an aisle of cubicles, most of them cluttered with family photographs. A belly laugh sounds from one of them.

"Here we are." She pushes open a door, decorated with a child's drawing. It depicts a man standing on a hill, his head twice the size of the sun. A tiny plane careens across the sky, painting the sky in bubble letters that read "Philandro Banks' Room."

A man sits inside, typing, his heels propped on his mahogany desk. Though it is easily six feet wide, it is bare except for a laptop, gum wrappers, and a bobblehead of Muhammad Ali.

"We've g-got a relative," the officer says in parting. "Here for suspect nine."

"Thanks," says the man, without looking up.

"Sir . . ." I clear my throat. "Sorry to bother you. I'm here for Franklin Baum. Seventy-four-year-old male, with a history of—"

"The shark whisperer," he interrupts, dropping his pen. "That's your old man?"

He props his elbows on his gut, fingers tented, regarding me with the friendly arrogance of a man who has seen worse.

"He's my father-in-law, yes."

"Well." He taps his fingertips together. "He's made my Saturday pretty interesting."

There is sarcasm in his face, but a trace of wonder, too. Pointing at his own cheek, he says, "You want some ice for that?"

"I'm all right, thank you. The important thing to know—"

"That was one mean umbrella," he interrupts. "Steel, he said?"

I nod. "He's bipolar, sir."

"So we heard." The corporal swings his heels off the desk, and the bobblehead quivers. "He's been easy. Connected us with his doctor as soon as he rolled in. Our psych team called her, recommended a thorough review. We can release him for the night, on the condition that he show up to All Saints Hospital by noon tomorrow."

He slides a document across the desk. Its heading reads Request for Emergency Admission.

"They'll keep him for a day or two." He laces his hands behind his head. "Then get back to us with an assessment."

"When would the trial be?" I say carefully.

He laughs. "I wouldn't get your hopes up. With psych cases, misdemeanor charges are usually dropped. Officer Shah filed the report. He'll brief you on the specifics."

A misdemeanor? I search his face for humor. Can he have actually written off the episode as vandalism, rather than the near multiple homicide it was? But there is no derision in his eyes, only impatience. He stands, glancing at the door.

The tank was not glass after all, but acrylic. So I learn in an interview room beside the holding cell, where Officer Shah—a lean man with stubbly jowls—spells out the damages: more than $5000 in repairs, likely covered by the aquarium's insurers. Even if he passes his medical review, Frank could face up to $1,000 in fines.

"These are just estimates," the officer concludes. "Their people are still evaluating the costs. In the event that they'll need to replace the tank, he'd be looking at a suit from their insurers, and a possible felony."

"He's already broke," I mutter, about to ask him how much jail time Frank will likely face, if he flunks his medical review, when the door opens.

Frank sidles in, escorted by the same officer who showed me to Corporal Banks's office. In the metallic light he looks fifteen years older. There is a reddish crescent on his wrist—from the handcuffs, presumably. His cheeks are pale, his hair still damp with rain. I cannot bring myself to meet his eye.

By the time we return to the parking lot, the storm has passed. Slow, tumid clouds block the setting sun.

"Where's May?" Frank says, as I start the car.

"With her dad," I reply, stung by the sound of her name. Again, the specter of what might have been rears up before me: water gushing from the tank, the floating strollers, the lacerated faces. *You could have killed her,* I do not say.

Frank fingers Maurice's sweater—spotted, now, with my dried blood. There is traffic on the freeway, so I take a longer route, through the outer reaches of Kingston.

"It wasn't speech," he whispers.

Then he is quiet, and after a while I wonder whether I have imagined the remark. We pass a pair of identical buildings, strung together by a laundry line that sags under the weight of one sodden, turquoise dress.

"You know how, in music, the notes go straight to the feeling," Frank says, "without wedging a thought in between? That's what their language was like."

"I don't know what you're talking about," I say, wary of triggering him again. But he continues, shamelessly.

"Everything they felt—it was written on their faces, in their gestures . . ."

We have reached an intersection. I brake, yielding to a slender man of Frank's vintage. He is dragging a suitcase, its little wheels accumulating slush. I nod as he raises a gloved hand in thanks, struck by the fact that the only thing standing between him and oblivion is the pressure of my sole.

THE STUDY OF ANIMAL LANGUAGES

". . . so in tune with one another," Frank is saying. "Their feelings—if that's what they were—they flowed through me. Beautiful, terrible dances of the soul, more exquisite than any thought of mine could conjure up. I felt oafish beside them, kid. Their joy was painful to me."

"You had a manic episode," I say.

"I swear to you." He turns to me. "I couldn't tell this to the officers, but I swear to you, I could hear—"

"What you heard came from your own mind."

Beyond the hanging traffic light, the old soap factory is coming into view. As part of an effort to gentrify the neighborhood, the state converted it last spring into a small museum. Prue and I took May soon after it opened, as part of our campaign to keep her occupied during her parents' divorce. Soap is made from lye and tallow, we learned, which comes from ash and melted fat. May had marveled at how two unclean things could be converted, through immense pressure and heat, into agents of cleanliness.

"I've never been surer of anything," Frank says. "I . . ." He drops the last syllable, pinching the bridge of his nose. With alarm, I realize he is crying.

"Animals protect their own kind," I say quietly. "So do we, and so should you. Learn at least that much from them."

His pocket buzzes. When he pulls his flip phone out of his pocket I feel an undertow of dread. Sure enough, he answers, "Pumpkin?"

She must be ready to crucify me. *First, he disparages my work,* I imagine her thinking. *Then he lets my father attack me, in front of all our friends. Then he almost gets my niece killed?*

"Not anymore . . . ," Frank says. He wipes his sleeve across his face. "We're in the car, yeah . . . A medical review . . . Saints, they said. Something like that . . . No, by noon tomorrow."

We pass an abandoned warehouse, laced with balding vines. A water tower looms above it, covered in graffiti.

"Uh-huh," Frank says again. "Okay. I love you."

He checks the phone, then says, "Hung up."

Snapping it closed, he lifts it up to shield his eyes. Light knifes through the windshield. The sun is still intact, hooded by clouds, like a huge fermata.

He says gruffly, "Just let me out here, would you?"

"What are you talking about?" I lower both our visors.

"I'll find my way."

"Where?" I laugh. "Back to our house?"

"To Vermont. I'll hitchhike." His voice cracks again. His hands are trembling. He sits on them, adding, "I've made enough trouble for you already."

I lock the doors, half expecting him to try to make a run for it. Instead he raises his chin, giving his head a little shake. The motion is barely perceptible, but it floods me with sympathy. That I have ever tried to argue with him suddenly strikes me as both callous and inane. He is too credulous, too hopeful. Like a child, he grips the edges of his seat—incapable, like a child, of rational thought.

"Do I really strike you as someone who'd help you break the law?" I say gently.

"Yeah, actually." He clears his throat. "You remind me of myself, sometimes."

THE STUDY OF ANIMAL LANGUAGES

I have to smile. The man really is out of his mind.

"You've got this energy in you," he is saying. "I can feel it. Always have. Just wish you'd let it out more often."

"You don't have to say that, Frank."

"I'm not buttering you up, I'm just—"

"And you don't have to like me, either. I can handle it. I wouldn't say we're exactly cut from the same cloth."

We turn east onto our street. Golden light swells in the rearview mirror.

"We're family," Frank says. "We're not supposed to like each other."

Our house is coming into view. The sun is low enough to accommodate the glow of lamplight from Josip's room upstairs, softened by a length of curtain. The blinds are drawn in our apartment, the kitchen windows dark. She must still be on campus. Thank god.

"I don't think I deserve your good graces, to be honest," I mutter, backing into the driveway. "Or Prue's."

Someone has shoveled the snow from the front path—Josip, most likely. Three snowmen guard our neighbor's lawn, in varying postures of surrender.

As Frank wipes his nose with his sleeve I hear myself say, to my own surprise, "It's true what you said last night. I was an idiot, shouting at her like that."

The words fill me with relief. Why deny them any longer? I will repeat them to Prue tonight, if she can bring herself to look at me.

"It's all right," he says. "It was a lot to swallow, what she said."

"No." I take a breath, then say in a rush: "What she said had nothing to do with it. Animals had nothing to do with it. It had to do with the fact that she's going places, and I'm going nowhere."

I unclip my seat belt, but he does not. He says, "You've lost me, kid."

So he wants me to say the words aloud. How generous.

"I don't know, Frank." I throw up my hands. "Maybe it's the fact that I still haven't published a book? Or that I peaked in my thirties, and she's just getting started? Or that my greatest accomplishment is a solution to a problem no one's heard of?"

He looks at me. I say, struck by the memory: "What you said in the rest stop the other day, about waiting? Waiting for life to happen to you, or whatever? Well, we have at least that much in common."

"But you're a philosopher," he says. "That's what she wants to be."

More like what you want to be, I think. But he is speaking again.

"I remember when she first called me," he continues. *"Dad, I'm dating this philosopher. He's brilliant. You're not gonna like him, which is exactly why I do."*

He unbuckles his seat belt. I stare at my lap, unnerved by this hint of all she must have confided in him about me over the years.

"You may be a goddamn pain," Frank says, "but you're a good person. A good uncle. A rock for Prue."

"That's an overstatement."

"You have a profession. More than that: a career. Enough fire in your belly left to still piss yourself off. Me?" He laughs ruefully, then gazes out the windshield—at the dumpster, or the elm behind it.

"Hell," he mutters. For a moment I am afraid he will start ranting again. But then he says, "I have no vocation. I don't even have a cause."

He opens his door, catching his sleeve on the lock. I reach over and pull it free.

"It's a good thing we're not cut from the same cloth," he adds. "For your sake."

Thirteen

————

I had forgotten about the flowers. They smell even stronger now than they did this morning, after stewing all day in the artificial heat.

"You trying to tell me I should become a gardener, Frank?" I say, locking the back door and flipping on the lights. "Because now I have no choice."

He chuckles. As I hang up our coats a rustling sounds from deeper in the house. I think I have imagined it, but then Prue strides into the kitchen, her expression fixed and dark. She must have been in here all along, I realize with horror, as she slips past Frank and angles toward me. I have the presence of mind to step back, turning slightly. While I had been ready for a smack, I am too stunned to feel either disappointment or relief as, stumbling over one of Frank's discarded boots, she reaches out and takes me in her arms.

"Walt mentioned you were hurt," she says, drawing back to inspect my cheek. "Here, come."

Still ignoring Frank, she leads me into the bathroom. Behind her body I see him shuffle down the hallway, toward the guest room. Then she closes the door with her foot.

"It's pretty bad." She sits me down on the lip of the tub, crouching before me. "But I don't think you need stitches. Let me just . . ."

She presses the skin beside the wound, and I flinch. She apologizes, and then lifts her hand up to the light. On the pad of her finger, moored by blood, is a splinter of glass.

"Hold on." She flicks it into the trash and then opens the medicine cabinet. She is wearing the silver pendant I bought her years ago, shaped like a wishbone, and her lavender fleece. Her phone is wedged into the pocket of her tight white jeans. As she rises on tiptoe to reach the highest shelf, I feel an erection coming on, despite everything.

She locates a pair of tweezers, swabs them with hydrogen peroxide, and then picks another shard out of my cheek. I wince again. As she murmurs her sympathy, echoes of our invective come hurtling back to me like shrapnel: *the bravest thing about you . . . the only thing we have going for us . . . crazier than your father.* Long ago, quoting a former teacher of hers during one of the marathon phone calls we had while she was on her Fulbright, she had described love as the act of teaching another person how to wound you most, and then agreeing tacitly never to do so. *You fail, of course,* she had added. *It's Chekhov's law: the planted weapon has to fire.* I asked her how she planned to do me in, when the time came, which was an early way of saying that I loved her. I don't remember what she said. I promised to throw at least one plate.

"I am so sorry," I say, as she smooths a bandage over my cheekbone.

"It's not your fault he went mental."

About our argument, I meant, but I do not correct her. Instead I tilt my forehead against her chest, inhaling her scent. Maybe this was all we had needed: a disaster to eclipse our own. As she strokes my back I close my eyes, allowing myself the facile thought that everything is relative, even catastrophe.

"In a way this isn't the worst thing in the world," she says. "Given that nothing irreversible happened. He needed a wake-up call. A stint in inpatient will do him good, I think."

I nod against her. Then I say, "I'm sorry about last night."

She sits back on her heels and sighs.

"It was pathetic to blow up at you like that," I continue. "Especially after your dad's—"

"Stop." She presses a finger to my lips. Then she says, with a mix of awe and consternation, "You really outdid yourself today."

She scrolls down my bottom lip, and I realize that she is referring to the flowers. My stomach flips. Yes, they really ought to have come from me.

"You never do things like that," she says. Then she leans forward and kisses me—softly at first, and then purposefully—like she hasn't kissed me in weeks.

I have to tell her, I think. She must sense as much, because she pulls back and studies me. Then she scratches at something on the underside of my jaw, blowing the powdery remnants—dried shaving cream, it must have been—off her fingernail.

"I miss you," I hear myself say. "I missed you today, I mean."

She makes a sound—half laugh, half sigh—and then kisses me again, almost angrily, her teeth scraping my lip.

I'll tell her tomorrow, I think, like a perfect idiot. It will be too late by then. I have no choice but to stop her. But I don't stop her, and before I know it we are making love.

I have lifted her up onto the sink, pulling her underwear to one side. As she arches her back the chain of extra links on her necklace swings back and forth, grazing the top of her spine. She moans, but in a canned way that makes me wonder with horror whether she is faking it. I draw back to find her eyes shut, her head tipped back against the mirror, patchy with my breath. I am still inside her, but we might as well be on separate continents. I try another tack, hissing her favorite obscenities, and soon enough her climax comes in four intensifying waves. She gasps, and I have to bury my face in her neck to keep from crying out as I give myself to her.

"I'm going to shower in here," she says. By the edge in her voice I can tell we have mended nothing.

She steps away from me onto the bath mat, wiping the inside of her thigh. "Can you bring me some fresh clothes?"

I fetch them for her, and then draw a searing bath that does nothing to make me feel cleansed. When I emerge she is still in the hall bathroom, though the roar of the water has gone quiet. I linger by the door, listening. No sound comes from inside.

"P?"

"I'll be right out," she says, too loudly.

I lean my head against the wall, toeing the strip of light where the bathroom tile meets the hall carpet. Then I say, "Can I heat up some food for you?"

"I'm fine." The sink faucet turns on. She adds, over the noise: "I had a late lunch with Daora."

They must have reconciled, then. I wander down the hall to check on Frank, feeling the familiar melancholy tug that follows reminders of the full life she leads independently of me—her other attachments, connections—and find him curled up in bed, his blinds drawn.

When I whisper his name, he doesn't move. He must be sleeping then, or pretending to, even though it is hardly past suppertime. Closing his door softly, I feed Rex, and then eat half a rotisserie chicken, letting the radio dull my thoughts. Already the memory of Frank's eruption is losing its patina, the crime itself seeming more absurd than barbaric. As the news segment yields to ads I think of the aquarium, its galleries dark, and of the life in its walls: the sharks moving silently behind the massive pane, its crack no more menacing than lichen.

PRUE IS ASLEEP by the time I reenter the bedroom and brush my teeth, but she has left the light on. Dalton's novel is tented on her chest.

A lock of hair has fallen across her nose and mouth, hewing to her lips with each intake of breath. Without touching her, I lift it up and lay it back across her pillow. Then I pick up the book.

There he is on the jacket, looking debonair as ever. City lights gleam at his back, and he is gazing into the camera, a smirk playing at his mouth as though he shares some secret with me. I wait for the twist of annoyance, but feel only exhaustion, mingled with guilt. The man could be gifted, for all I know. And so I flip to a page near the beginning, which Prue has dog-eared.

————

She must still love him, she thought, because she loved his qualities. They hadn't changed. She almost never wished they would, and when she did she retracted the thought, or replaced it with a memory of when things had felt natural between them. She handled them lightly, these memories, taking care not to dwell on them too long. If she did, she might notice in one of them a flaw, or flatness, a detail successfully forgotten, that if remembered would disqualify the memory, throw the whole scene out of key.

One day her confusion had resolved itself into a sentence which, despite its initial shock, had calmed her. It came to her loudest when he climbed into bed, or when the lights of his approaching car swung across the kitchen wall. She learned gradually to keep it at bay, the sentence, but all the same it had become a kind of anthem.

He made her sad. That was the sentence. It was so simple she had almost laughed aloud when it first came to her. A sentence as humble as that—four words, four syllables—must have a cure. There was another sentence, after all, with which it coexisted: She loved him. It was all a matter of uniting the two sentences, she thought, of finding the right conjunction. She tried them out: He made her sad *but* she loved him; he made her sad *because* she loved him; she loved him *although* he made her sad.

Perhaps they had simply become too adept at playing the roles they had created for each other, she thought. Perhaps that was all: they had grown tired of the roles. She tried to think of a way to say this, without sounding harsh or unhappy, and could not. The roles had been traded in silence. Besides, she was no longer sure of the margin between herself and the character she assumed with him, of whether such a margin still existed.

Their lovemaking had been thrilling, then tedious, then resolute. It was curious, she thought, how solitary the act could be, each body working toward its separate end. For all she knew, it made him lonely, too. It was no one's fault. It was possible that this loneliness was a condition of the altered love that awaited them, later in life. They would feel for each other a new and quiet warmth, she imagined, consisting in their having acknowledged their failure to disclose themselves to one another, and forgiven it.

"What do you think?" Prue says.

"Jesus, you scared me." I close the book, losing her place, and hand it back to her. Then I turn off my lamp.

She is still looking at me. Only when I slide down under the quilt do I realize that I have not answered her question.

I say, "I didn't get far."

She blinks, and my throat tightens. Can she have seen herself—ourselves—on that maundering page?

"It's fine," I add. "A bit ponderous, though."

"Yeah," she says, after a moment. And then she puts out her light.

Fourteen

A siren wakes me up just after dawn. Prue is still sleeping. Our legs have entangled, and as I disengage she mutters something. The sound frightens away the memory of my dream.

The light is on in the hall bathroom. Although Frank's toothbrush—its bristles fried—is jutting off the edge of the sink, I hasten toward his room, fearing the worst. He had wanted to hitchhike home yesterday, after all. What would have stopped him from slipping out in the night?

But when I reach the threshold I find him inside, perched on the sill of the bay window. His T-shirt is tucked into his corduroys, his hair combed back. He is scribbling something on a legal pad.

"You're up early," I say, my heart still thrashing.

He lifts his pen, startled.

"Can I make you some breakfast?" I say.

"I helped myself, thanks."

He smiles. He has stripped the bed. The sheets are on the carpet, gathered in a neat white mound.

"I'll be in the study if you need anything," I say, and he nods.

As the sun rises I sail through Natasha's latest chapter, impressed—as usual—by the clarity and vigor of her prose. Then, partly to assuage my guilt at having lied about them by omission, I use a large measuring cup to water each of the flowerpots Frank ordered. By the time I have reached the nineteenth pot, containing yellow tulips, Prue is awake.

"Ready, Dad?" she says, when I return to the kitchen. Her voice is tight. She cracks the knuckle of her pinky, waiting over the drip cone as her coffee percolates.

Frank nods, already bundled in his coat. He is sitting at the table, staring down at an uneaten bowl of raspberries. His copy of *The Nation*, flipped to the last page, lies beside it, along with Prue's leather gloves.

"I have some errands to run afterward, but I should be back before dinner," she says, as I refill the measuring cup with tap water. Then she swings the sodden filter into the trash, holding her palm underneath it to catch the dregs.

"I'll cook," I say as she flinches, blowing on her open hand.

May's flower juts from the outer pocket of Frank's bag, its tissue petals torn from the party.

"I want to say something to you both," Frank says abruptly.

Prue catches my eye, alarmed. I move to her side.

He stands up and takes a faltering step back, almost tripping over his shoelace. Then he says, "I am so very, very sorry."

He looks at her, and then at me. Prue glances my way again, but I am too embarrassed for him to meet her gaze.

"You're competing with the maestro of apologies," she says.

With a bolt of dread, I realize that she has outed me about the flowers. But Frank doesn't pick up on it.

He says, "I just have one favor to ask you."

"What is it, Frank?" I jump in, relieved to push the conversation elsewhere.

"Please . . ." He presses his lips together, drops his eyes, and then faces us again. "Would you take me to jail, instead?"

"Jesus Christ." Prue turns and flings open the refrigerator, removing a carton of cream and pouring a liberal dose into her coffee. Frank watches her in desperation.

"You're the one who told the cops about your diagnosis," I say softly.

"I know I did," Frank says, "but I've thought about it, and I'd rather bite the bullet."

"*Bite the bullet,*" Prue mutters, shoving the carton back in the refrigerator.

Frank adds, "I want to pay for what I did."

"Don't bullshit me," she says. "I know you're just trying to avoid your meds."

He squares his shoulders, but the tremor in his chin gives him away. So that's what this is about. As he draws a deep breath, I feel a fresh wave of remorse at how dismissive I had been about his pills. The poor man is ill. I should have seen it years ago.

"Why did you come here?" Prue says suddenly.

He opens his mouth, but before he can reply she says, "I told you not to, didn't I? I told you to stay home."

Frank blinks. "I wanted to hear you deliver your speech." When she rolls her eyes, he adds: "It was a beautiful speech."

"No." She laughs bitterly. "You wanted to upstage me, is what you wanted to do. Well, congratulations, Dad. It worked."

"P . . ." I murmur. I have never seen her speak to him like this. Frank is staring ahead dully.

"You devastated May—*twice*," she continues. "You humiliated me. You *kicked* me?"

Frank winces.

"It may come as a surprise to you, Dad, but you're not a prophet. You're a provocateur."

"You're right," he says.

She screws the cap onto her travel mug—too hastily, because it jams. She curses, trying again.

He adds, "That's why I belong in a cage."

With a groan of frustration, she braces the heels of her hands on the counter, letting her head hang between her shoulders. I set down the measuring cup, pick up her mug, and screw the cap on for her in silence.

Finally she says, "You don't belong in a cage."

"I do," he says.

I hold the mug out to her and she grabs it, moving past Frank to yank her coat off its peg. He follows her with his eyes.

"I'm not sick," he says. "I'm just a lousy person."

"Dad . . ." Her voice is trembling now.

"Why don't I drive him?" I say. But she shakes her head.

"I'll be in the car," she says, and turns away from us, forgetting her gloves on the table.

The door slams. Besides Frank's breathing, the only sound is the crunch of her footsteps on the gravel.

"Can I give you a snack for the road?" I say, to fill the silence.

Frank shakes his head, and then fishes in his pocket. He produces a sheet of yellow paper, folded twice in half.

"For May." It flutters in his hand. "Promised her a story. Would you give it to her, if you have a chance?"

"Of course," I say. Outside, the engine chugs to life.

"I was going to call her last night, to see how she is. "She gets bad dreams, you know." He scratches his neck. "But now, who am I kidding? I'm the nightmare."

The car horn blares. Frank glances at the floor, and then crosses one leg over the other, gritting his teeth as he reaches toward his shoe. Realizing that he is trying to tie his lace, I crouch down and do it for him.

"She'll understand," I say, when I stand up. "At least when she gets older."

He manages a smile, and then limps toward the door.

"You should really take something for the road," I say on impulse. "Crackers? Cheese?"

"I'll be fine," he says, and opens the back door. Wind rushes into the kitchen, turning a page of *The Nation,* which he has not bothered to pack.

"You have a ways to go," I say.

He hoists the strap of his duffel bag over his shoulder. "Agreed."

"I meant—"

"Thanks for putting up with me this week, kid," he interrupts. "I owe you."

"You don't owe me anything," I say. But he is already closing the door softly, his footsteps lost in the voice of the engine.

Once upon a time there was a town. Now this was a strange town, May, because it didn't actually exist. But that wasn't the strangest thing about it, actually. The strangest thing about this town was that you would never know, looking at it, that it was out of the ordinary! It looked perfectly normal. There were houses in it, and clouds, and lots of mailboxes.

Anyway, the point is that everything about the town felt nice and firm and solid, and that only deep, deep down did the townspeople suspect that it might not be as solid as it looked. That was a dangerous thought, they knew, but they weren't sure why. Once in a while, someone would gather the courage to speak the thought aloud. "If this town exists, where is it?" she might say. When somebody said a thing like that, it was taken as a joke. People found it funny at first—some people—but not if the person kept on saying it. If she did, she was given pills to take. The pills buried the thought.

The reason for the pills was simple. Only without the thought could the townspeople carry on with the day. Carrying on with the day was what most of the townspeople meant by "happy." The only way to be happy, therefore, was to bury the thought.

The problem, though, was that burying the thought planted a terrible sadness in the townspeople. The sadness was so distracting that most of them forgot its connection to the thought. They forgot about the danger of asking what was strange about the town. They even forgot that the town was strange. Instead, their minds were taken up by a new thought: "Why am I sad?"

THE END

That's a shoddy story, bug, but it was the best I could manage today. I bet you can think of a better one. Would you tell it to me, someday?

I'm thinking of you every minute, May. I am so sorry.

Love,

Grandpa

A vibration drones behind me. I turn, Frank's page in hand, and have to dive forward to stop Prue's cell phone from shuddering off the counter. She must have forgotten it, I realize, glancing out at the empty driveway. On the screen, still lit, is Dalton's name.

The phone is still buzzing in my hand. Paralyzed, I silence it, and then wait to see if he will try again. When he does not, I wake the phone, enter Prue's passcode, and check her missed calls. At the top of the list, above my own name, Adaora's, and Walt's, are the words "Dalton Field" in scarlet. He has called her twice.

I have no desire to confirm my fears, nor to hear his voice, so it is with some surprise that I find myself calling him back.

I hold the phone a safe distance from my ear, then wait. Two rings go by. On the third, he picks up.

"Sweetie," he says. "I'm running to a book event, it's stupidly early. . . . *Shit*—" a horn sounds behind him, the scratch of tires—"but I wanted to see if you were free later tonight? Darling? Are you there?"

Part III

————

Fifteen

—

For a long time I remain still. There are things to do, such as wash and dress and eat. There are many things to look at besides the phone, which, after hanging up, I have placed on the counter. There is, for example, the radio, and the drying colander, and the knives. They have not moved. They have not changed, even though they appear brand-new.

The clues were everywhere. They rush toward me, incontestable, like iron shavings under the organizing force of truth: That dog-eared page. The joyless sex. The scuffling in the background, when I called Prue yesterday. His absence at our party. Their banter during her Q and A. Her willingness to sabotage her tenure case—and run off with him, presumably. The unfamiliar necklace. The figure in the trees, when Frank and I pulled into the driveway Thursday night. Her itch for Germany. The rift. The way he looked at her. *The way he looked at her.*

He calls back. I press Decline. Then, without hesitating, I drop her phone into the full measuring cup. It bounces against the glass base, releasing a few tiny air bubbles, and brings the water level flush with the spout. Then, somehow, it vibrates again, sending tiny waves splashing onto the counter.

I run to the sink and wretch. Nothing comes up, so I spit. My saliva engulfs a stray poppy seed and ferries it down the drain.

I should be screaming or swearing. Weeping, at the very least, though I haven't cried in years. But I feel no sadness. Only a wrenching in my chest, mingled with nausea, as though my lungs were climbing into my throat.

Her gloves are still on the table. So are her books. Her mail. Her scent. The whole house reeks of her. I reek of her.

I grab my briefcase from the study, pull on my down coat, and burst into the cold. The sky is overcast, but the sun is burning through the clouds. I am still in my pajamas—sweatpants and a T-shirt—but it doesn't matter. There will be no one in the office, and I cannot bring myself to face our bedroom.

As I crest the hill leading to campus I remember that the logic exam is due tomorrow morning, the same time as the Philosophy Department's biweekly meeting. The thought soothes me, in its normalcy.

My usual route to the Philosophy building is still fenced off, thanks to the oil leak, so I circle around the dining hall. A group of athletes are trickling in, visibly hungover. Mirthless laughter sounds from inside.

"Apollo!" a familiar voice calls out. "Apollo, stop!"

From behind me comes a bright, jangling sound, followed by huffing breath. I turn to find Quinn's golden retriever nosing my ankle.

"I thought that was you." Quinn joys toward me, reining in the leash as Apollo's snout travels up my shin. She catches her breath. "How are you?"

She is wearing spandex, sneakers, and a neon pink thermal shirt, shadowed with sweat at the neckline.

"Fine, thanks," I say. *My wife is having an affair.*

"He's still learning his manners." She glances at Apollo, who is sniffing at my crotch. As I reach down to derail him she adds gently, "I spoke to Prue last night. She took me through everything that's happened."

I stare at her, horrified. Can she know? She must. Everyone must.

But she says, "My sister's bipolar, too."

So she had been referring to Frank. The party, the aquarium, Frank's arrest. How distant all that seems.

"How is he now?" Quinn says.

"Better," I lie, and bend down to scratch Apollo's chin. He tilts his head, ears cocked, mouth steaming. *Isn't it strange,* Prue once said, *how in a town containing hundreds of dogs, you almost never hear a bark?*

"I know Prue's a little concerned about her speech," Quinn says.

As she speaks, I realize that she is beautiful. There is an elegance, and a trace of mischief, to her face, with its high forehead and limpid green eyes. What would it take, I wonder dumbly, to run away with her? What would I have to say?

"I would be, too," she continues. "It wasn't exactly conventional. But I told her, as I'm sure you have, that it was marvelous."

There is a note of challenge in her voice. Prue must have told her about our fight. *If only she knew,* I think. So I tell her.

"Prue's cheating on me."

Her eyes widen, and I feel a stab of vindication, adding: "I found out about fifteen minutes ago."

She opens her mouth to speak, but nothing comes out.

"I should have seen it coming, frankly."

"I . . ." She glances at Apollo, who is licking mud from the side of my shoe. "I can't believe it. I'm so sorry, Ivan."

A group of coeds bluster out of the dining hall, chattering. As they stream around us—one of them reaching out to tousle Apollo's ears—I say, "I'm on my way to my office now, to put some things in order. I'd love to sleep with you sometime, by the way."

Her eyes almost pop out of her head. I turn and hurry toward the philosophy building, feeling strangely exhilarated. Astonishing how easy it is after all, to say precisely what you feel.

I unlock the main entrance and jog up to my office on the second floor, taking the stairs two at a time. The door of the reading room—where we gather for department meetings—is open, but there is no one in the kitchenette, and no sound except the wheeze of the photocopier.

My shock is thawing, now, into a rancid ache. *Coffee,* I think fiercely, anything to crowd out the ghastly fragments: *sweetie . . . darling . . . free later tonight?* They bombard me nonetheless, and I curse under my breath, approaching the counter of the kitchenette to find the electric kettle already on. I freeze, listening. My colleagues' doors are shut. Down the hall the copier throbs on, drily.

"Professor Link?"

Natasha Díaz leans out of the reading room. She is wearing a blue floral dress, cut low in the front to reveal a spray of freckles across her cleavage. Her lips are redder than usual.

"Didn't think I'd see you here." She smiles. *Any chance you'll be in your office this weekend?* she had asked, at our party. *Fuck.*

"I was just finishing up last week's problem sets," she says. "Do you want them?"

"Sure," I say, and she ducks back into the reading room. I pour myself a cup of instant coffee, my heart in my ears.

"Thanks for your comments on my chapter," she says when she emerges, handing me the graded stack. Over her shoulder I see that she has spread her books, a bottle of chocolate milk, and a Tupperware—flecked with the remnants of her breakfast— across the round table. Her viola is propped against a chair.

"I think I answered my own question, from before," she continues, "but there were just a couple of comments you made that I couldn't read." She rummages in her handbag, producing the rumpled pages and glancing at my office door, just across the way from the reading room. "Do you have a second?"

"I have all the time in the world," I say, too loudly, because she hesitates.

To set her at ease I turn and unlock my door, suddenly grateful for the intrusion. The ache in my chest is yielding now, to rising fury. By comparison, anger feels like a relative of joy.

"Is Professor Baum's dad okay?" Natasha ventures, as I toss my coat over my swivel chair.

Frank's outburst at the party, she must mean. She has managed to sound concerned, though the glitter in her eyes suggests otherwise. What delicious gossip we must have given her.

"He's not, actually." I sit down on the edge of my desk.

Her eyes roam down my body, and I remember what I am wearing. She has rarely seen me without a blazer on, let alone in my pajamas. I fold my arms over my T-shirt, feeling my chest hair pricking through the thin cotton.

I say, "He's being checked into the hospital as we speak."

"I'm so sorry." Natasha shifts her weight, then adds falteringly: "Is there anything I can do?"

I chuckle. "Just bring that here." I gesture at the chapter in her hand. "Let's get this over with."

Like a lapdog, she obeys, hovering by the bookcase as I clarify my scribbled edits. When I am finished I say, "Can I ask you something?"

She glances at my bandaged cheek. Her hair is gathered in a heavy braid, so glossy it looks wet.

Without waiting for her reply I say, "What attracts you to this stuff?"

"To Wittgenstein?"

"To philosophy."

She bites her lip. Then, to my surprise, she answers in earnest: "I don't know. It speaks to me, I guess. I'm sure you can understand that."

She smiles at me, and I realize that I have no idea what she is talking about. Whatever passion drove me from Boston to Albuquerque to Rhode Island, into the farce of a tenured professorship— *the freedom to say anything, now that you have nothing left to say!*—has long gone cold. But what does it matter, now that my marriage has gone up in smoke?

I clear my throat. "You're smart, Natasha. You're a delightful person. I gather your parents are wealthy."

Her smile fades.

"The average readership of an academic paper is 0.6," I continue. I had come across the figure somewhere. It is probably false, but it is certainly true for mine. "If you're lucky, your papers will earn you tenure, and you'll get to spend the rest of your life talking to yourself."

"Are you—" she begins, but I interrupt her.

"As for me"—my heart is pounding again, but it only spurs me on—"I could have done something with my life. I could have stood for something, or someone. Instead I'm standing here, wasting your time."

"Are you having a midlife crisis, or something?"

A question, a provocation. She regards me candidly. Watching her, I am suddenly tired of pretending obliviousness to the fact that her questions—sincere, intelligent—are also ways of flirting.

"Because I think you're a great professor," she says.

There is a trace of down on her upper lip. She smiles again, shyly, and I decide to call her bluff.

Sixteen

Relationships between students and faculty members have been banned at the College for decades. Of the three professors caught breaking the rule, two have been fired. No untenured professor would dream of returning an advance, and—even among permanent faculty—only an imbecile would make the first move.

I become that imbecile. In an instant I have pushed Natasha against the bookcase, freeing a small primer on Kant. It skims her shoulder before landing on my foot, and as I kick it off I press myself against her. My heart is beating in my dick, which has risen to the occasion, so full it is almost in pain. Her lips are softer than they look. I plunge my tongue between them, feeling a frisson of relief at counteracting Prue's betrayal. Then I grab a fistful of her hair and kiss her neck and collarbone, at which point I realize she is speaking.

The words drift toward me, as though through fog: "Wait . . . please . . ."

I draw back, still clutching her hair, and take her gaze like a bullet.

"Oh no . . ." I hear myself say. "Oh god."

As I stumble back against my desk she flattens herself against the bookcase, gulping air. Her face is white.

"I'm sorry." I force myself to look her in the eye. "I don't know what came over me."

Still fighting to catch her breath, she stares at me in terror. There is a halo of lipstick around her mouth.

I bolt out of the room, down the stairs, and out of the building, dodging Clarice Hussein, who calls after me. Her voice propels me across the road and into the main quadrangle, where a few students are sledding on trays filched from the dining hall. Watching them, I suddenly forget why I have come to campus. Then, feeling the lightness in my arms, I remember my briefcase. The logic exams. Though my phone is still in my pocket, I have left them upstairs, along with my coat. There is no question of going back for them. Not now—and perhaps not ever, depending on how Natasha chooses to handle my behavior.

A sound leaves me—less a shout than a whimper of incredulity—materializing as a cloud of vapor. I curse, shivering, as much to bury the sound as to rekindle my anger. Sure enough, the rage returns, fiercer than before, and then I am back in motion, my ears ringing, crossing the quad in ten huge strides. I take a sharp left, still running, not so much planning where to go as reading my intentions from the movement of my feet.

The chapel bell tolls. I am close to elation now, less and less able to deny where I am headed, though I have almost no chance of finding him there.

The English Department shares an entrance with the Student

Union, which is open. I swerve into the atrium, past the Center for Community Service and café, weaving around a group of students. One of them—Jacob, from my logic class—waves to me. I charge past him, sprinting up the stairs toward the offices above.

There is still time to recover myself. The part of me I recognize is urging me to turn back, gather my things, and book a hotel. But that would force me to assess the damage I have caused, and I have fallen too far now to keep from plunging further.

I find his door beside a restroom, at the end of a dim hallway. "Dalton Field," reads his nameplate. I stare at it, collecting myself. Then I knock three times.

Silence. I hold my breath, scouring the quiet for the sound of him. On the phone his voice had sounded far away, steeped in the noises of urban rush. Though he is teaching this semester, I cannot picture him frequenting this musty corridor. Berlin or New York, maybe, but not here. Inside the neighboring office someone coughs.

The knob gives in my hand. He must be inside, then. I open the door.

Light streams through the windows. There are towering shelves, a broadloom, a floor vase printed with Fabergé eggs. No Dalton, however. His leather chair is empty. His desk consists of a broad, converted door, bearing a spiral-bound calendar. In the corner is a plant with fleshy, succulent leaves. There is a samovar beside it, mounted on a teak credenza. The air smells faintly of mint.

A scuffing sound comes from the hallway. I slip inside and dodge behind the samovar, but it is only his colleague next door, locking up. She retreats down the hall, whistling to herself, and then her footsteps echo from the stairwell.

It is then that I remember what he'd said on the phone—
something about a book event. I dart behind his desk, scanning
for clues. Today's leaf of the calendar reads "Reading @ Bart's,
Noon." The bookstore: Prue's favorite spot in town. My watch
says 12:37. It must be under way, then, just down the road.
Through his window the shop is almost visible, tucked between
the movie theater and the green cornice of the town hall. A five-
minute walk, at most.

I arrive in two. A blown-up cover of *Forgive Me Not* dom-
inates the glassed-in display, surrounded by hardbound copies
of the thing. I push the door open slowly to avoid sounding
the entrance chime. It tinkles anyhow, and a few people glance
my way.

Dalton is stationed behind the music stand the bookseller
has set up in lieu of a lectern. Harsh white light illuminates him
from a spotlight mounted on the ceiling, its glow diluted by the
daylight coming through the front windows. The sleeves of his
Oxford shirt are bunched up near his elbows, revealing two
muscular forearms. The seats before him—arranged around a
center aisle—are full.

"Not every day, though," he says, and grins.

Laughter swells from the audience, and I take my position
behind a chair in the back row, where a grizzled man is cro-
cheting.

"Scout's honor," Dalton adds. Then he scans the faces, gripping the stand like a sprinter about to vault.

He must be taking questions, then. Perfect. I raise my hand.

Dalton squints. "Hey . . . Ivan, right?"

The smile he offers me is confident, postcoital. Nonetheless, he has not succeeded in disguising a ripple of tension along his jaw.

Three dozen faces turn toward me, expectant. With a dash of fear, I wonder whether Prue's is among them. It isn't, of course.

"I was hoping we could do this in private," I begin. "But it looks like that won't be possible."

A few people stir, but Dalton only frowns. The poor thing must be dizzy with fear.

"We both know you have something to tell me," I say. "I have a question about your novel, in the meantime."

He cocks his head. A born philanderer. His wife will find out soon enough.

"The marriage you depict in the book," I say. "My question is, who inspired it? Your wife, or mine?"

People are murmuring now. The grizzled man sets down his yarn.

"I can't tell," I say, "because, rather than expose the vicissitudes of love—as you clearly hoped to do—or anything whatsoever about the human beings involved, your prose does nothing but conjure up a vague sense of ennui that feels more masturbatory than anything."

The bookseller stands up. So does a plump, red-faced man in the first row.

"Whoa," Dalton says, as though speaking to a horse. "Can we back up?"

Not quite an admission of guilt—not yet—but enough to drive me up the aisle, buoyed by adrenaline, and by the strange and repugnant sense that my transgression with Natasha has united us.

"I disliked you from the moment we met," I say, nearing him. "I found you arrogant and gauche. Your wife . . ." Remembering my Google search, I add, "Robin, is it? I doubt she'll even be surprised when she finds out."

He backs away from me, tripping over one leg of the music stand. The red-faced man steps between us, but I evade him, close enough now to smell Dalton's cologne.

"Let's slow down for a second, okay?" he says, raising his hands.

"I'll slow down when you stop fucking my wife."

"Holy *shit*," a young voice whispers. Someone calls out, "Stop that man!"

There is a general rustling, and as I grab Dalton by the wrists I half expect the crowd to rise up and charge me as one.

"I think you are referring to me?" the red-faced man says. He glances from me to Dalton and back, pointing a short, dimpled finger at his chest. Despite his thick black hair, he looks north of fifty, with a shiny forehead and pouchy blue eyes.

I tighten my grasp on Dalton's arms, but he makes no effort to free himself.

He says, "This is Robin, my husband."

"You'd better work on your alibi," someone bellows.

The voice is mine. Nevertheless, I have the curious impression that it has come from someone else, someone vivid and invincible, who might as well be dancing as he winds up and strikes Dalton across the face.

Seventeen

———

My solution to the Gettier problem rests on a thought experiment. To the question *How can we really know anything, if we cannot rule out the possibility that our knowledge might be true simply by chance?* I pose the following case: an archer draws his bow in a thunderstorm, aiming it at a passing hawk. Though his technique is poor, the wind carries his arrow to the bird, which falls dead.

Knowledge is like this. Beliefs may be accurate, in other words, but for all the wrong reasons. They may be inaccurate, on the other hand, for all the right ones. Yet the Gettier problem dissolves if we shift our focus from the relation of a given belief to chance—represented, in the thought experiment, by the relation of the arrow to the wind—to the skill of the archer. The question *Is the belief justified?* yields to another: *Can the knower be trusted?*

"... husband of that scientist I was telling you about," someone is saying behind me. As he speaks again, I realize it is Dalton.

"You know, Prue, the one who gave that speech?" he adds, and another voice murmurs in recognition. "Yeah. The one I was calling on the way here."

My cheek is squashed against the complete poems of Elizabeth Bishop, my wrists locked in place by the bookseller's moist hands. After I smacked Dalton, he shoved me against the wall. The side of my palm is still stinging from the impact.

"Do you think he's on something?" someone murmurs.

There is a silence. From the corner of my eye I see a few audience members lingering near the doorway of the shop, snapping my picture with their phones.

"I'll call the police," the bookseller says. "Should I call the police?"

"Just let me talk to him," Dalton replies.

"I'm not so sure—"

"Don't worry, I won't sue."

The grip around my wrists relaxes, and I turn to find Dalton sitting on a vacated chair in the front row. The red-faced man has crouched down before him, cradling his face. Dalton's upper lip is swollen.

"You're not seeing her?" I hear myself say.

"I don't play for that team, my friend," Dalton says. He starts to speak again, but then something occurs to him. "Wait . . ." His eyes narrow. "Was that *you* on the phone this morning?"

I make no sign of affirmation, but he says, "*That's* why—" Then he cuts himself off, glancing at the red-faced man. "Babe, I just realized what happened."

"This fucker hit you, is what happened," the man says. Softly, he blows on Dalton's lip.

The words echo back to me: *My husband, Robin.* Can it be?

"Prue—I thought she hung up on me, remember?" Dalton is saying. He stabs his thumb in my direction. "*He* did."

"You know this person?" the bookseller asks Dalton. He glares at me, adjusting his suspenders. We have met in passing, once or twice, but he must not recognize me. I can hardly blame him.

"I certainly don't," Robin says.

My limbs are tingling. The ringing has reentered my ears, so I barely hear Dalton answer, "I do. There's been a misunderstanding."

He is still studying me in disbelief.

"I thought . . ." I manage to say, but it comes out as a wheeze.

All three of them stare at me, waiting. Their schadenfreude is too much to bear.

I scuttle toward the door, prompting the few remaining onlookers to flatten themselves against the bookcases. Then I head back across campus, down the hill, and up our street, jogging, and then running, to keep warm.

Our car is in the driveway. Prue must be back from the hospital, then. I burst in through the back door, so cold I can no longer feel my hands. Her drowned cell phone is still in the measuring cup on the counter, like a fossil from another world. She is probably showering, or in the study. Though I know it won't be possible, at least for long, all I want to do is hold her.

First I turn on the kitchen faucet, running my fingers under warm water. They are just beginning to thaw when a floorboard groans behind me.

Prue says softly, "What were you thinking?"

She must have heard by now. If Dalton had texted her—and he probably had—the message would have come through on her laptop. Or maybe he'd called her on the house phone. And if not him, someone else. Chances were good that she'd had at least a friend of a friend in the audience.

I turn, drying my hands on my sweatpants. She is standing in the threshold, still dressed in the sweater and dark jeans she was wearing this morning. Her arms are folded across her chest.

"I don't know what came over me," I say. My voice—nasal, querulous—horrifies me, but I press on. "I thought I'd lost you."

"Mission accomplished."

I have never seen her this angry. Her voice has dropped in pitch. Whatever happens, I can tell that it will be necessary to proceed very carefully, disguising every advance as a concession.

"I should have been open with you," I say. "But I've felt so distant from you lately, and I"—my voice is trembling, but her gaze does not waver—"I was a coward."

Through the window, I catch a trace of motion. Josip is scattering salt on the steps leading up to his apartment, a dead cigar between his lips.

"You're still managing to make this about you," Prue says. "It's amazing."

She picks up one of the smaller flowerpots, containing daffodils, then adds, "I commend you. Seriously."

"The point is . . ." I take a breath. "I slapped him. That's all. It was terrible, but that's all. I'll go apologize. Right now, if you want. I'll do anything. Whatever it takes."

Her face drops. "Wait, what?"

"He didn't tell you?"

"Dad?"

Josip's door closes above us. I freeze.

"You slapped him, too?" She gives a strident laugh. "Unbelievable. Un-fucking-believable. What the hell is wrong with you, Ivan?"

She tosses the pot in the air, and then catches it, sending clumps of soil flying.

"Just tell me one thing," she says. "When were you planning to tell me?"

"I'm sorry, I don't—"

"Were you *ever* planning to tell me?"

"I don't understand."

"Nope, you weren't. You were never planning to tell me that these"—she brandishes the pot—"did not come from you."

She hurls it against the refrigerator. With a bang, it splinters in two, scattering soil across the room. The daffodils flop against the tile.

"Shit," I exclaim, involuntarily.

"Shit is right," she says. "Don't you realize they're the only reason I *slept* with you last night? All part of your plan, wasn't it? And this morning"—her voice breaks—"this morning, when you watched me screaming at my father, you knew he'd nearly blown his credit limit on me? You sick fuck."

I open my mouth, and then close it. There is nothing to say. She is right.

"And that's not even the worst of it," she continues. "We arrive at the hospital, after he's apologized for not adding *orchids* to the mix, and I learn that his last pill was administered by you, at three a.m. Saturday, when you apparently intercepted his attempted *escape in our car?*"

"I didn't want to worry you," I whisper.

"You've never patronized me, Ivan. Don't start now."

"You're right, I'm—"

"Why didn't you tell me?" Her voice buckles again, and she opens her arms. "I'm your *wife*."

I bite the insides of my cheeks. My face is working in ways I cannot control.

"I knew things were bad between us." She wipes her eyes. "But I didn't think they were this bad."

"P . . ."

"Do you know what it's like, being married to you?" she says suddenly. "It's like wearing a fucking straitjacket. I wake up beside you sometimes, and I ask myself, what was I thinking?"

"I bought us tickets to the Galápagos," I blurt out.

She squints through her tears. *"What?"*

"It was supposed to be a surprise," I say.

Her nostrils flare, and then she frowns. "What is that on your mouth?"

I touch my bottom lip, confused, as she adds, "Is that *lipstick?*"

"Yes," I say. The truth is all I have left.

"This is a joke," she says under her breath. "This is some sick—"

"You forgot your phone this morning," I interrupt. "Dalton called. The writer? I picked up. From what he said I thought you were sleeping with him. I . . ." I catch my breath. She is still staring at me, the fury in her eyes fading to disbelief. "I confronted him at his reading. Worse than that. I hit him. And before that, I kissed my TA, Natasha?"

She steadies herself against the counter.

"I thought it would neutralize things between you and me, or something," I continue. "I don't know. I can't . . ." I put my face in my hands.

"What's happened to you?" Prue says faintly.

When I face her again she is pale.

"I'm sorry about the flowers," I say. "I was going to tell you, I just—"

"I'm calling Adaora." She backs away from me, glancing around the room.

"I'm sorry for shouting at you, on Friday. I'm sorry for—"

"Where did you put my phone?" She is prowling the kitchen now, kicking a shard of ceramic under the stove. With a flicker of dread, I remember where it is—soaking there in the measuring cup, right in front of her.

"Where did you *put* it?"

I step between her and the counter. But she ducks behind me to check the key caddy and, as she turns back, sucks in her breath.

"Oh my god." She glances from the cup to me. "*What* did you . . ."

Unable to face her any longer, I grab my coat from the mudroom. And then I am sprinting back over the snow and sunny ice, in no particular direction.

Eighteen

Only once I reach the harbor do I begin to cry. The sobs are dry at first, some of them painful. And then tears come, like sweat from a broken fever.

I have wandered east down a network of side streets, and then along a bike path adjacent to the highway. When I reached the exit for the state beach, I veered off, across an intersection, and down a few back roads, ending up on a parkway that overlooked the sea. I walked along it until I found an underpass, and followed that to a wharf—a hive in summer, no doubt, but empty now except for a few gulls, scattered lobster traps, and a dock bearing a sign for a ferry to a nearby lighthouse.

I lower myself onto a bench facing the sea. There is no one else in sight, and no sound except the occasional wash of cars. It must be close to dusk, because a pale moon is rising in the east. A gull keens. The ferry hangs from a girder, its belly stained with seawater.

The lighthouse blinks in the distance. The land around it is studded with young, denuded trees. Two of them walk off to-gether suddenly, and I realize they are not trees, but a couple. From this far away, their gestures seem involuntary.

I have always believed there is a comfort to be found in de-spair: namely, from the knowledge that, like a pendulum at its extreme, one is simply gathering momentum for the reversal, the plunge back toward a mood of possibility. If happiness can be tempered by the knowledge that it won't last, then surely the op-posite is also true. For that reason, I have sometimes found it possible to revel in melancholy, just as I am sometimes able to wallow in physical illness. But the misery I feel now is of a differ-ent grade. For the first time, I cannot muster my usual trust in the promise of a complementary swing. It is as though the instru-ment itself has changed, or stopped.

My lungs ache. When I have no tears left, I lean forward and rest my head between my knees. As my vision clears, a patch of coarse, wet grass resolves between the slats of the bench. Nestled in it is a spherical, thorny object. I reach down and pick it up. It is a husk of some sort, resembling an oversized burr. I close my fist around it, firmly enough to feel a bright, uncomplicated sting. When I open my fist, four dots of blood bloom on my palm. Against my misery, the pain feels almost like pleasure.

Something vibrates against my thigh. My phone, signaling an incoming email. I pull it out of my pocket and stare down at the screen, waiting for the marks to resolve into words.

"RE: Book Proposal," reads the subject heading. It is from Angela Axel, editor in chief of Cornell University Press.

"Dear Ivan," the preview reads. "This is unusual for us, but I wanted to let you know that I read your proposal overnight. It's . . ." There the preview ends.

I open the email. It continues: ". . . excellent. I'm blown away. I'm still waiting to hear from one of our editors, but consider this a tentative yes. Let's talk by phone? AA."

On impulse, I press Forward and type Prue's name. Then I stop myself and reread the message. Here it is, the news I've always dreamed of, and I cannot even tell her.

I CALL A CAB HOME, hoping she will be there, but only Josip's car is parked in the driveway. There is a note on the kitchen counter, held in place by a bowl of dried rice. One corner of her phone peeks through the kernels.

"Went to Walt's," it reads in her terrible handwriting, which I have always loved. "Need some time."

The broken pot is still lying on the tile. Dirt radiates out from it in all directions. The daffodils, clinging to hunks of soil, slump against the refrigerator.

I rescue the flowers and sweep up the dirt. Then I gather the shards of ceramic, wrapping them in paper towels so they won't scrape the young man who collects our garbage. When I am finished, I take a long shower.

The moon is bright by the time I emerge. I draw the bedroom blinds and peel the soaking bandage from my cheek, leaning close to the mirror to inspect the wound. The angriest part has scabbed over, the new skin flaky with moisture. I find a fresh bandage in the hall bathroom and cover it again, less dexterously than Prue had. There are rings under my eyes, but other than that my face looks the same, somehow: my thin mouth and lantern jaw, my long nose, my chin with its old acne scar. I turn off the light, not bothering to pause, as I usually do, to check whether the lines in my forehead have deepened.

I have eaten nothing all day, but I have no interest in food. Nonetheless, I force down a banana and some toast, and then—after feeding Rex—pull a fresh sheet of paper out of the printer.

"Dear P," I write. "There are no words to express how sorry I am. I have been a terrible husband to you."

True, but false. I start over.

Dear Prue,

I don't know how things have come to this. But I do know that I have no more lies left. I'll start at the beginning.

Your father was florid when I drove him home on Thursday. We stopped at a diner, and he kept going on about your finches. He even grabbed our waitress—not sexually, but still. I gave him the car key and told him to go get his meds, and he went out to the parking lot. When he came back inside, he said he had taken them. I thought he might be lying. I didn't tell you.

He was still manic a few hours later, when he woke me up in the middle of the night. You were sleeping. I came into the living room and found him banging the ceiling with a broom to stop Josip from practicing. I took it away from him and he went back to bed. I didn't tell you that, either.

In the kitchen, during our party, he fumed to me about how nobody "got" your speech. I didn't warn you. That was a few minutes before his first outburst.

At two o'clock the next morning, our car pulled out of the driveway. I didn't wake you. Frank was driving to Noboru's to apologize. I stopped him and, as you now know, watched him swallow one pill's worth of Clozaril.

When we spoke the next day, I didn't mention the incident. I didn't even tell you about his gift. You wondered aloud whether a zoo was the best place to take a manic vegetarian. I took him there anyway. I took May, too.

I cannot imagine the horror and anger and disbelief you must feel at having been lied to, in these multiple, unforgivable ways, by your partner—especially given that, had you known the truth, perhaps your father wouldn't be in the hospital right now, your rib bruised, your niece traumatized.

What was I thinking? I wish I knew. I can't bring myself to imagine that I wanted this to happen, but maybe you were right: maybe, on some level, I wanted to undermine you. It's not always easy being married to someone so talented, and with so much courage. Let's just say your speech hammered that home to me.

I know I have to apologize, but I don't know what to say. I lie to you, attack your friend, and cross the line with one of my students, and "I'm sorry" is supposed to cover that? Is

*that supposed to mean anything to you? I can understand
why you wouldn't accept it.*

Though I don't deserve it, I hope you'll come home.

Love,
Ivan

I type the letter up and email it to her as an attachment, copying Walt in case she deletes it. In the body of the email, I ask after May.

Then I take a sleeping pill.

Nineteen

————

There is a new face at the department meeting the next day: Peter Chao, a philosopher of mind, on leave from Peking University. Though his research appointment begins in January, our chair has invited him to this meeting—our last of the semester—so he can get a feel for the rhythm of things.

It took all my will to get out of bed this morning. Nonetheless, I replied to the editor at Cornell, turned in the logic exam, and forced myself to campus in time for the meeting, refreshing my inbox every few minutes to check for a reply from Prue.

"You were in a hurry, yesterday," says Clarice Hussein, as we settle around the table in the reading room. She adds, smiling, "I don't think I've ever seen you run before."

Only then do I remember that she had intercepted me on her way into the building yesterday afternoon, as I bolted from my office. Natasha must have shown herself out after I left, and then returned to her dorm room or—hopefully—to a friend's. The memory of her stricken face fills me with shame.

"Didn't mean to embarrass you," Clarice whispers.

"It's not your fault," I assure her, and the business begins.

On the agenda is a preliminary review of the finalists for our postdoctorate position, followed by a reopening of the debate our resident historicist sparked during our last meeting, about whether to expand our course offerings to include classes on non-European thought, a notion I found reasonable. Barring that—and here I had disagreed, though I couldn't care less anymore—we should consider renaming ourselves "The Department of Western Philosophy."

". . . a lot to offer," Rhonda Patel—our metaphysician—is saying, referring to the postdoctoral candidate. "But I don't see him linking this stuff to broader trends."

Dominic Kensington, our Hegelian, murmurs his assent. "We don't want too much overlap, besides." He pats my shoulder. "We've got our epistemologist."

I smile. Partly out of shyness, and partly to respect the preference I have always assumed they share for segregating work and life, I have never made much of an effort to befriend my colleagues. Nonetheless, they have always been kind to me. When, on an impulse, I solicited their advice about a paper submission on our department listserv, each of them responded—most within a few days' time—with thoughtful comments. At our annual holiday party, when the accumulated cost of my reticence is most conspicuous, they and their spouses go out of their way to make me feel included. Late last year, when I got tenure, almost all of them sent me congratulatory notes.

They fall silent now, staring at me. We have been going around the table, I realize, sharing impressions of the candidate's dossier.

"Sorry." I riffle through his CV. I reviewed his application last week, marking my comments in the margins, but am suddenly unable to decipher them.

Feet shuffle. The radiator ticks. My annotations might as well be gibberish.

"I don't know," I say, and look up.

There is an awkward silence, broken by Gordon Cage, our chair: "Didn't get to it?"

I shake my head. "I read it. But I don't remember what I thought about it anymore. I'm sorry."

As people shift in their seats, Gordon says, "Okay, then. Clarice, what did you—"

"My book is getting published," I interrupt.

They stare at me.

"That's fabulous," Rhonda says at last. Peter, our newcomer, glances around the table.

I add, "Cornell's putting it out."

"Try to sound a little less excited," says Dominic, prompting a round of warm, nervous laughter.

"I want to thank you all for something," I say, cutting it off. I take a breath. "I know I've never been an especially generous presence around here. I'm self-involved. Not good with people. And you've extended yourselves to me anyway, more than I deserve."

Marsha Petrov, our ethicist, locks eyes with Clarice.

Rhonda says, "Ivan? What is this about?"

"Sharing a department with all of you has been the highlight of my career." I stand up. "I wish I'd made more of it, when I had the chance."

I gather my briefcase and coat.

"Hey!" Marsha calls after me, but I am already on my way out the door.

Downstairs, I shrug on my coat, pull out my phone, and call a cab to All Saints Hospital.

Twenty

M orning visiting hours have ended by the time I reach the psychiatric ward, but the receptionist offers to check with the attending physician to see if they can accommodate me. He takes my name, pointing me toward a waiting area flanking the bolted yellow door.

When Walt calls I pick up immediately, thinking it might be Prue, but then his voice comes through the earpiece.

"Hey, man. I think you cc'd me on something by mistake?"

"I just wanted to make sure it got through to Prue," I say. "You can read it, if you want."

"Don't plan to," he says. From the gentleness in his voice, I know she has told him everything. "Anyhow," he continues, "you asked about May? She's home sick today, but she's been a champ. She's right here, if you want to say hi."

"I'd love to."

There is a rustling, and then May's voice says, "Uncle Ivan?"

"Yes sweetie, it's me. How are you?" I fish in my briefcase for Frank's story, thinking I might read it aloud to her, and then remember I have left it at home.

"Are you sleeping over, too?" Her nose is audibly stuffed up.

"Aunt Prue went to work, but she said she's coming back to-night."

"I wish I could, but I—"

"You have to see my new glasses!"

"New glasses already? No way. What color?"

"One sec, I'll show you the picture my dad took." There is a silence, and then I hear the swoop of an outgoing text. A moment later, my phone vibrates.

The image shows May sprawled on her living room rug, smiling tentatively. The thick, circular frames on her new glasses make her look like a young teenager. I zoom in, studying the surroundings for any trace of Prue. A peach comforter is draped over the couch cushion, seemingly dented by some recent, human weight.

". . . same ones Harriet wears," May is saying, when I lift the phone back up to my ear. Harriet the spy, she means.

A shadow darkens the frosted glass square in the door of the ward. With a hitching sound, the heavy lock slides out of place, and then a man with blond sideburns pokes out his head.

"Ivan?" he says. I wave to him. "Franklin's ready for you."

"They're even cooler than Harriet's," I say into the phone. "Look, May, I have to go, but feel better soon, okay? I'll be thinking of you."

The man shakes my hand as I cross the threshold, introducing himself as Nurse Harris. A small gold crucifix hangs at his throat.

I follow him down a corridor lined with pale blue doors. Some of them are open, revealing figures reading or napping. A few of them look up as we pass.

We turn left into a rec room filled with tables and plastic chairs. A shaft of light slants through one tall, barred window, broken by an elderly woman standing before it, gazing out. Several other people—old and young, male and female—sit at the tables, two of them playing cards. In the corner is a counter stacked with plates, half obscuring a chalkboard that reads "Lunch: Beef Stroganoff."

"He'll be right in," Nurse Harris concludes. He adds, grinning: "Character, your dad."

I do not correct him. As I sit down at a free table, the woman turns from the window, and I have to stop myself from gasping. Thick black marks are scrawled across her cheeks.

When she sits down, I discover their source: a Sharpie, which she pulls out of her pocket, along with a pocket mirror. She opens the mirror and then, with great care, writes the letter Z on her forehead.

And then a figure is shuffling into the room, his hair wet from the shower.

"Frank." I stand up to greet him, relieved. "It's good to see you."

He accepts my embrace but does not return it. He is wearing a smocklike shirt I do not recognize, printed with tiny blue wheels.

"How are you feeling?"

"Fine." He lowers himself into the chair across from mine. "Docs say I'm off the hook for a felony."

"Really? That's wonderful."

I swallow, struck by how frail he seems. His eyes are glassy, his face bloated. There is too much to say.

"I'm sorry to show up like this, out of the blue," I begin. "But I wanted to apologize."

"What for?"

He is pausing before each sentence. The delay is subtle, but definite enough for me to scoot closer to him, taking his soft, papery hand in mine.

"A lot of things," I say. "First of all, for not telling Prue you ordered the flowers. I let her think they were from me—I'm sure she told you. I'm ashamed."

Frank squints, as though chasing a thought.

"And about what an asshole I've been to you this week," I continue. "You're not well, and I haven't taken good care of you. I've even provoked you, and I'm sorry. I can't tell you how sorry I am."

The scent of beef is filling the room. There is an ambient, clinking sound.

"You look different," Frank says.

I wait for him to say more, but he does not. His nose twitches. His stubble is coming in white.

"I destroyed my life," I whisper.

A nurse appears with two plates of slippery pasta, interspersed with lumps of beef. After serving a young woman, she sets the remaining meal down before Frank.

He picks up his fork. I expect him to limit himself to the noodles, but then he stabs a hunk of meat.

"Frank . . ."

"Yeah?" He licks the gravy off the tines, and then feeds the hunk into his mouth.

"What are you doing?"

"Eating," he says, through his mouthful.

"That's beef."

He lifts another forkful to his face.

"You don't eat that." I scan the room for the nurse. Instead I catch the eye of the woman with the Sharpie, who winks at me.

I stand up, raising my voice: "You're a vegetarian, remember?"

He shrugs, regarding me dimly. There is a desolate composure in his eyes.

"Someone?" I call out. "Is there a doctor, here?"

The woman lets out a long, toneless cry. As it intensifies, Nurse Harris hastens back into the room.

"Please . . ." I intercept him, gesturing at Frank. "Can you get him something else? He doesn't eat meat."

"Looks like he's enjoying it just fine."

"You don't understand . . . ," I begin. He glances over my shoulder at the woman, who has fallen silent.

"He would never do that, ordinarily," I say.

The woman cries out again, and the nurse pushes past me.

Desperate, I kneel down before Frank, who seems oblivious to my efforts.

"Let's get you out of here," I say.

He mumbles, "I'm in the middle of lunch."

"Let's get you home." Before he can eat another bite I take his face in my hands, his soft skin pooling over my fingers. Beige liquid dribbles from his mouth.

"Sir?" comes a female voice. I register the livid clop of heels, and turn to find a woman in white.

"Franklin?" she says, leaning toward him. "Is this man bothering you?"

"Yeah." Frank wipes his mouth with his sleeve. "He's family, though."

She glances at Nurse Harris, but he is tending to the woman. To me she says, "Visiting hours are over, sir. Please come with me."

Without another word, she takes my arm and steers me back into the corridor. Frank bends over his plate, still chewing patiently as I am swept away.

Twenty-one

I call a cab back to campus, asking the driver to book it. But there is a traffic jam on the highway, and the trip takes over two hours. By the time we reach the science building, the western sky is flaming with light.

"Thank you," I say, and tip him liberally. Then I dash up to Prue's office.

Her door—covered with May's drawings—is locked, so I try the Center for Ornithology, my heart sinking. She must have driven back to Walt's already.

But when I reach the aviary I find her sitting inside, alone, visible through a glass panel beside the door. The staff member usually stationed here must have gone home for the day, because the reception window is dark. A poster for her lecture is still taped to the wall, featuring a blown-up image of a finch. It stares into the camera with its bright black eyes, the branch beneath it embossed—by a trick of Photoshop—with Prue's name.

I knock, and she meets my eye through the glass. Her face registers no anger—only surprise, mingled with sorrow. She is perched on a director's chair in the balmy, winterized portion of the lab, under an imported tree. Two branches, wrapped in leafy vines, hang from the ceiling. A small gray bird flits between them.

"I'm sorry to interrupt," I blurt out, when she opens the door. "I'll leave if you want. I've just come from the hospital."

She is dressed in her teaching uniform: a blazer and black jeans. She looks at me.

"I went to see Frank." I rake my fingers through my hair. "To apologize."

She seems older, somehow. The finch chirrups overhead.

"Come in," she says.

I follow her into the soft, damp air of the enclosure, raising my voice over the birdsong: "It was chilling to see him there, P. I know he needs it, but whatever they have him on—lithium, or something?—it's . . ."

Wordlessly, she offers me the director's chair, but I sit down on the grass instead.

"We spoke this morning," she says, looking down at me. "He sounded fine."

"He's not in pain, or anything. And he's not manic. But he ate beef." I stare at her, but she only blinks. "Can you imagine?"

I shield my eyes against a sunbeam coming through the glass wall. It faces the dense, outdoor portion of the center, reserved for local birdlife.

"I'm sorry." I turn my back to the sun, the cool grass sticking to my ankles. "I'll go. Do you want me to go?"

Instead of replying she sits down, too—not on the chair, but on the ground, cross-legged, facing me. Her hair is piled in a messy bun, looking especially golden. Behind her, the sky is bluish pink, the strong light sharpening the edges of the chapel and campus center.

"I read your letter," she says.

Her voice is quiet. Under ordinary circumstances, I would think she had drifted into one of her wistful moods—usually triggered by too much work, or too little sleep—that usually culminate in tears.

"Things have been bad for so long," she says. "How did we let this happen?"

"How did *I*," I say. "It's my fault."

"No." She stares at her hands. "I've been shutting you out for a long time." Tracing the lines of her palm she adds, "I was scared. It felt so unfair—how the things you lived for were making me feel trapped."

There is a scuffling above us, and a leaf twirls through the air, coming to rest on the inside of her thigh. As she folds it once, and then again, I say, "You could have told me, P."

She gazes up into the branches, where a pair of finches are pecking at each other. "I've been so lonely with you," she says.

I take her free hand, stroking the back of it with my thumb, but it stays limp. "I've been lonely, too," I say.

She has folded the leaf into a tiny bundle. When she places it on the grass between us it expands, the new seams glowing with sunlight. She says, "Did you actually buy us a trip to the Galápagos?"

I nod. Then I ask, "Why did you marry me?"

She laughs, but it comes out as a sigh. "I've been asking myself that a lot lately."

The comment stings, despite its legitimacy.

She says, "Do you remember that fight I had last winter, with Daora?"

I do, vaguely, but before I say so she continues: "It was about you, actually." She swallows. "I was over at her place for drinks one night, when Edson was traveling, and we were talking about you two. I said something about Edson that annoyed her, and she retaliated by saying she had no idea what I could possibly see in you. *How do you live with that man?* I remember her saying. *He's very handsome, yes, and smart, but so buttoned up, to put it generously. Probably even on the spectrum.*"

A finch lifts off the tree and settles a few yards away from us. Twittering, it ducks its head, its orange beak vanishing into its downy chest.

"You should have seen her face when I told her what you've done." She smiles, despite herself. "She didn't even believe me until she'd heard from Dalton. And even then—"

"She was right," I interrupt. "There's something wrong with me."

"Oh, stop it."

"I don't deserve you."

"You're just shy."

"I'm a walking punch line, P. I specialize in knowledge, and I'm clueless."

"I'm not much better." She nods at the finch. "Thinking I can talk to him, when I can't talk to my husband?"

The bird has swiveled around to prune its wing, but now it freezes, its throat palpitating, though it makes no sound. It stares through the wall of the laboratory, at the middle distance, where a small crowd is feeding into the chapel.

Prue says, "Did you really proposition Quinn?"

I wince. But her eyes sparkle.

She says, "It's a little bit funny."

To my surprise, she scoots forward and crawls into my lap, startling the finch. Faint with gratitude, I wrap my arms around her.

"I've missed you," she says into my chest.

"I'm right here."

"Now, maybe." She tilts her face up to mine. "But come on. We've both been out to lunch."

I blow a stray eyelash off her cheek, and she squints, adding, "I wasn't having an affair, but I may as well have been. *You* may as well have been. You knew that. You must have felt it."

"I don't feel it now."

"We should have seen this coming." She smooths the loosening edge of my bandage. "I mean, think about it. You want to hole up with your proofs. I want to travel. I want to show that language is bigger than we are. You want to reduce it to math. Minus the sex, we're a match made in hell."

"But we're married," I say. "You're the love of my life."

"We drag each other down though, don't you think?"

The finch is hopping toward us. When it reaches my foot it hesitates, inclining its head. Then, with a complicated whistle, it swoops back up into the branches.

"Just imagine," Prue says. "You'll never have to clean up after me. You can leave parties when you want to. You won't even have to go to them in the first place. You'll never have to hear another word about animal—"

"No," I interrupt. "P, no. Stop."

"You're in your forties," she whispers. "You'll find some-one else."

She smiles bravely. Her eyes have filled with tears.

She says, "You can even start a family if you want."

"You are my family."

I take her face in my hands. Her eyes are dark and wet. I feel a reckless pull toward her body, stronger than any other wish.

She says, "I accepted the fellowship."

"What?"

"At the Max Planck Institute. I wrote to them this morning."

I tip my forehead against hers. If I can put enough time be-tween myself and her words, it might be possible to believe I have imagined them.

But now she is speaking again, drawing away from me, sitting up: "It'll be good to get some distance from this place, whether or not I end up getting tenure. And besides, we need some time apart."

A trial separation, she does not say.

"What happened here?" she says suddenly, holding up my palm. The four cuts from the wharf have scabbed over.

Instead of replying I reach for her, struck by the question of how she will die. Cancer? A ruined car? Time has always been kind to her. I picture the deep laugh lines, the soft white hair.

"You're the best thing in my life," I say.

She is quiet. The finches sing. We hold each other, no longer speaking, until the sky goes dark.

Twenty-two

Prue moves a box of her things to Walt's on Wednesday, and on Thursday I resign from the College. After recounting my behavior with Natasha to the dean, I mail two letters of apology to her and Dalton. Then I drive Frank—who has been discharged from the hospital with a new prescription and, thankfully, no fines to pay—back to his home in Vermont. Prue had offered to do it, but I insisted, and there had been no argument.

Frank lives in the converted attic of a shingle-style house, walking distance from town. When we arrive I follow him up the three flights of stairs, prompting a symphony of creaks. Prue and Walt have been trying for years to find him a more practical arrangement. Last spring, he finally agreed to see a first-floor studio several miles away, but he hadn't liked the smell, and besides, it was too far from the library.

"Warmer today," he says.

It amazes me that, after all we have been through this week, we can still talk about the weather. When I tell him this, I expect him to come back with some riposte—*when we talk about the weather, we're never talking about the weather*—but instead he gives me a funny look.

As we step inside, Frank's cat, Cordelia, leaps off of the futon. I have offered to help him set out a week's worth of food for her, since his knee still prevents him from bending down.

She trots over to us, already purring. When I scratch under her chin, the sound deepens. Her yellow ear—torn at the tip, from her years as a vagabond—folds over as she nuzzles my shin, closing and then opening her eyes.

"She puts up with me," Frank says. "Even though I'm a goon that can't hunt."

While he pours me some water, I shake out three bowls' worth of food pellets, setting them beside the automated drinking fountain Frank bought for her. Other than that new addition, and Cordelia herself, the apartment looks the same as it did on my last visit, three years ago, with Prue and May. Books dominate the space, stacked in slanting towers. Before the futon is a glass coffee table filled with curios. There is a tiny phonograph, its horn sprouting a four-leaf clover, and a set of anthropomorphized chess pieces. Beside them is a fragment of a wildebeest's skull Prue smuggled back for him from the Serengeti, and an album of Frank's honeymoon with Nadia.

I open it. Frank appears, occasionally, but the photographs are mostly of her. Nadia wrapped in Spanish moss, shielding her eyes against the sun; Nadia smelling bougainvillea; Nadia in a city square, drinking from the mouth of a stone lion.

"You sure you're feeling okay?" I say, when he hands me my water.

On the drive up we had been mostly quiet, listening to part of a blues album Frank dug out of his bag, and then to NPR.

"Says the guy who got himself kicked out of a psych ward?" He grins. "Folks were still talking about it yesterday. A regular McMurphy."

I take a sip, studying him. The bloating in his cheeks has faded. His gestures are still sluggish from the lithium, but the old glimmer is back in his eyes.

We still have three songs left on the album, so before I leave Frank loads it into his CD player. When he collapses beside me on the futon, Cordelia leaps onto his knee, turning three circles before curling up between us.

The last song ends and the player clicks off, but we keep on sitting there. I pet Cordelia, following her gaze to a triangle of sunlight inching across the spine of one of Frank's tomes.

Finally I say, "Would you like to come to the Galápagos with me?"

He has tipped his head back against the cushion, his eyes closed. Realizing he has fallen asleep, I wonder whether I should wake him up before I leave. As I start to ease off the futon, however, he opens one eye. "Serious?"

"I have the tickets," I say. "For two weeks, starting January third. One of them was for Prue, but . . ."

He reaches out and squeezes my shoulder. She has told him everything.

"I'd love to." He strokes Cordelia's head. "But what would this one do while I'm gone?"

"True."

There is a rush of wind outside, and the room fills with light. Something small and hard hiccups down the roof.

"This is all you," Frank says. "Take yourself on an adventure. Who knows, you could be the next Darwin."

Voices filter from the stairwell, sprinkled with laughter. Frank's neighbors, probably, coming in from the cold.

"It's funny," I say. "I've been alive for almost half a century, and I don't know the first thing about anything."

"Amen." Frank slaps his knee, rousing Cordelia.

"I used to think . . . ," I trail off. "I used to think life would go like this: You get bashed around a bit, fuck up, lose people, and in the process figure out what really matters. But now . . ."

He sips from my water glass.

"It's more like figuring out that your life was never even about you, to begin with. You're not the hero. You're just some-one in the cast."

"I'll be damned," Frank says. "You're starting to sound like a philosopher."

Before I leave he insists on arming me with snacks for the road. I accept them, and then pet Cordelia goodbye.

"Will I see you again?" I say, straightening up.

He stares at me, surprised, and then claps me on the back.

"What kind of bullcrap is that? I'll be knocking at your door before you know it, kid. You'll be sick of me."

I let him hug me, and then put on my coat. He walks me back downstairs.

It is close to evening, but the light is stronger now than it has been all day. As I make my way to the car Frank falls back, wav-ing. His shadow stretches all the way down the block.

"Don't be a stranger," he shouts.

I raise my hand.

He is still standing there when I reach the car. As I open the door his reflection swims across the glass: backlit, blazing, like some Icarus. Though I do not turn around, I can feel him watching me as I climb into the driver's seat, wake the engine, and begin.

Author's Note

Ivan's solution to the Gettier problem was inspired by Ernest Sosa's work on the subject. The abstract of the paper Ivan peer reviews was adapted from Özlem Beyarslan and Ehud Hrushovski's paper, "On Algebraic Closure in Pseudofinite Fields," published in 2012 in the *Journal of Symbolic Logic*. Prue's study on birdsong was inspired by Kentaro Abe and Dai Watanabe's paper, "Songbirds Possess the Spontaneous Ability to Discriminate Syntactic Rules," published in 2011 in *Nature Neuroscience*.

Acknowledgments

Whoever said a happy childhood was the worst gift to give a writer never met my family. For their love and enthusiastic support, I would like to thank my parents, Glynnis O'Connor and Douglas Stern, who read every single draft of this novel. My beloved sister, Hana, sustained me with her humor and bullshit allergy, and by putting up with the sound of my typing in the early mornings.

For enabling me to throw myself full-time into the initial drafting of this book, I would like to thank the Thomas J. Watson Foundation, especially Chris Kasabach and Sneha Subramanian, and Denise Gagnon and Suzanne Spencer at the Amherst College Fellowships Office. For the time and space to destroy and rebuild it, I am indebted to the Iowa Writers' Workshop. I would like to thank my teachers, Lan Samantha Chang, Paul Harding, Benjamin Hale, Charlie D'Ambrosio, Kevin Brockmeier, Ayana Mathis, and Alan Gurganus for their wise and meticulous reading; the Susan Taylor-Chehak family and the Maytag Corporation Fellowship Fund for their support; Deb West, Jan Zenisek, and Connie Brothers for their generosity of spirit; and my peers, Sorrel Westbrook, Shaun Hamill, Mgbechi Erondu, Erin Kelleher, Jason Hinojosa, Joseph Cassara, Monica West, Kris Bartkus,

ACKNOWLEDGMENTS

Nyuol Tong, Melody Murray, Iracema Drew, Amanda Kallis, Maya Hlavacek, Keenan Walsh, Sasha Khmelnik, Ryan Tucker, Patricia Helena Nash, Liam O'Brien, Regina Porter, Okwiri Oduor, and, especially, Maria Kuznetsova for their encouragement and solidarity.

The Writers' Workshop is also where I met my inimitable agent, Henry Dunow, who saw this novel through multiple transformations. Without his editorial eye, insightfulness, and moxie, it would not exist in its current form.

For their feedback on early drafts, I am tremendously grateful to Roger Creel, Carolyn Ruvkun, Brian O'Connor, Nica Siegel, Andrew Zolot, Kate Johnson, Gerry Howard, Jareb Gleckel, and Eskor David Johnson. Thanks also to my teachers at the Brearley School, Amherst College, and Yale University; to Shakespeare and Company bookstore for its hospitality; to the Franke family; and to Yale's Comparative Literature Department for its ongoing belief.

To everyone at Viking who put this book into the world: my gratitude knows no bounds. On the production end, I would especially like to thank Gretchen Schmid, Allie Merola, Elizabeth Yaffe, Gretchen Achilles, Eric Wechter, and Trent Duffy for his exquisitely thorough copyediting. On the publishing side, I am enormously grateful to Andrea Schulz, Kate Stark, Lindsay Prevette, Chris Smith, and Brian Tart. Most of all, I am indebted to the wonderful Lindsey Schwoeri for her patience, incisive questions, and dazzling editorial powers.

J.M. Coetzee's novel *Elizabeth Costello* inspired some of this book's subject matter. For the conversations that also fed it, or for advice at a key juncture, I would like to thank Shruthi Badri, Chelli Riddiough, Viveca Morris, Taylor Grant-Knight, Sofia McDonald, Maru Pabón, Rick Stern, Lisa Djonovick, Joanne Gillis-Donovan, Pedro Reyes, Danielle Amodeo, Terry Cullen, Asja Begovic, Henrik

ACKNOWLEDGMENTS

Onarheim, Jennifer Acker, Patricia Morrisroe, Lee Stern, Sarah Aubrey, Solyda Say, Allegra di Bonaventura, Ayesha Ramachandran, Moira Fradinger, Marta Figlerowicz, Martin Häglund, Phyllis Granoff, Alexander George, and John Durham Peters. Special thanks to my dear friend and sparring partner Deidre Nelms, whose enthusiasm for this project never flagged despite the many drafts I foisted on her; to Lenka Peterson and the late Ruby Stern; to the O'Connor and Stern clans; to the Barsh-Garbasz and Silver-Greenberg families; and to my Brearly Squad, the antitheses of fair-weather friends.

While they did not have a direct hand in this novel, Daniel Hall and Adam Sitze supplied the wisdom and mentorship that informed its growth. I am deeply grateful to both of them. I would also like to thank Susan Sagor for her early confidence and outstanding intellectual example, and for introducing me to the semicolon.